Because of Grace

Because of Grace

Book Two

Loretta Sorensen

prairie hearth
publishing, llc

YANKTON, SOUTH DAKOTA

Because of Grace

ISBN: 978-1-969893-04-9

© 2025 Loretta Sorensen: Prairie Hearth Publishing LLC

Cover art: Prairie Hearth Publishing, LLC

Interior: Prairie Hearth Publishing, LLC

All Scriptures taken from the New International Version (NIV), unless otherwise indicated.

Published by Prairie Hearth Publishing, LLC
2310 Willowdale Rd
Yankton, South Dakota 57078

Dedicated to my mother,
Gertrude Marie Stainbrook,
and countless numbers
of others who have provided light
along my own pathway to find
the priceless treasure that is
God's mercy and grace.

Table of Contents

CHAPTER ONE

Embers of Grace

The late-morning sun streamed through the single window in the kitchen, casting a warm glow over the rough-hewn table where Keri set the letter. It lay beside the cloth and burlap bags of flour, coffee, and oats that she picked up at the general store earlier that morning.

Neatly penned on a crisp envelope of cream paper, its edges slightly creased from the long journey from Wyoming Territory to their Dakota Territory homestead, was "Mr. And Mrs. Karl Richmond." Obviously, Gran's careful script. The ink was bold against the dust-smudged paper. Keri's fingers lingered on the words, tracing the edges, her heart quickening with a mix of curiosity and dread. Gran had promised to write, and Keri and Karl were anxious to hear news of Karl's father, Alex, and the ranch. But Keri wouldn't open it, not without Karl.

She turned back to the iron stove, where a pot of beans simmered lightly, the faint scent of bacon grease mingling with the cook-stove woodsmoke. She glanced up and down the kitchen shelves, lined with supplies: colorful jars of recently harvested vegetables, pickled beets, a sack of sugar, and a tin of flour Karl had hauled from the general store last month, which was still half-full. It would take some reorganizing of jars, sacks, and tins to find a spot for the new supplies purchased just this morning. The simple task helped take her mind off the letter, which loomed like a threat. Its contents, coming from Gran, a steady source of wisdom and godliness, may be simple enough, even joyful. Or . . . even her unspoken thoughts caused Keri's heart to thud with a warning rhythm.

She glanced at the letter again. It was postmarked nearly two weeks ago—no sign of tear-smudged ink or dust. The name and address gave no hint of scribbling or haste in their application. So much could happen in just two weeks. Keri's own life story was a testimony to that. Whatever the letter's contents, she must patiently wait for Karl to come in for dinner before it could be opened.

She stirred the beans, her movements mechanical, her mind tethered to that letter. Outside, the wind rustled the dry grass as it carried the distant whinny of horses and squawk of hens as they foraged for their morning fare. Karl would be in soon, boots heavy with dust from the barnyard, his face lined with the quiet determination that had carried them through so many challenges these past months. How would they weather the one facing them now?

The door swung open right at noon. Karl stepped inside, wiping dust from his face and clothing with a faded bandanna. His broad frame filled the doorway; his homespun shirt, patched at the elbows, carried the marks of many of the chores he'd completed since early morning. "Smells good in here," he said, offering a tired smile as he hung his hat on the peg by the door. His eyes caught the letter on the table, and the smile faltered. "From Gran?"

Keri nodded, drying her hands on her apron. "Mr. Purdy says it came with the morning stage. Addressed to us both. He figured it hadn't been at the store more than an hour before I stopped." She kept her voice steady, but her fingers twisted in the apron's hem, betraying her nerves. She struggled to find a few words that would ease the tension overtaking them both. "Gran promised she'd write."

Karl's jaw tightened, and he crossed the room in two strides, his boots thudding against the worn pine floor. He picked up the envelope, turning it over as if something on the back might reveal its contents. "I guess we'd better read it," he said, half to himself. He glanced at Keri, his hazel eyes searching hers for a moment, then pulled a pocketknife from his trouser pocket and slit the envelope open. The flap tore open with a sound like ripping silk, releasing a chill draft of foreboding. Was it bad news? The first line would likely tell.

Keri stood close, her shoulder brushing Karl's as he unfolded the letter. Gran's handwriting filled the page, neat but hurried, the words spilling out like she'd written them in one breathless go. Karl read aloud, his voice low and steady at first, then catching as the news unfolded.

"Dear Karl and Keri," he began, "I pray this finds you well. I'm sorry to send such tidings, but things aren't going well here. Karl, your father's taken a turn for the worse. The consumption has worsened, and the doctor

10

says there may not be much time left. He's clearly too weak to work the ranch anymore, and from what I can tell, we'd better sell the ranch before the bank takes it over. I know this may cause some hardship on your part, but you need to come as soon as you can to help with the ranch. Both of you should come if possible. Alex needs to see you, Karl, and we need to talk about bringing him back to the homestead. We all know the risks, but I can't bear to send him away to die alone. Come quick as you're able. You know God is with us all. Your loving Gran."

The words hung in the air, heavy as the late summer clouds now suddenly gathering in the west, blotting out the warmth of the sun. Karl's hand dropped, the letter crinkling in his grip. Keri reached for his arm, her touch light but firm. "Karl . . ." she started, but the words caught in her throat. She saw the weight settle on him, the way his shoulders squared even as his face paled.

"Pa's been sick a while," he said, staring at the letter. "I thought we probably had more time. Maybe in spring . . ." He shook his head, folding the paper and tucking it into his pocket, as if hiding it could lessen the truth. "The ranch always was his pride. If it's failing, it's killing him faster than the sickness."

For a long moment, neither of them spoke. Keri broke first, her voice hoarse with emotion. Keri broke first, her voice barely above a whisper.

"He's your father, Karl. He raised you after your mother was taken. He taught you how to break a horse, how to be a man, and how to stand up straight when everything inside you wants to fall." She looked up, eyes shining. "I owe him for the man you are. We have to bring him home. We do."

Karl pushed off the sink and crossed the room in two strides and cupped her face in his rough hands—hands that had never been gentle with much of anything except her.

"Keri." His voice cracked on her name. "If I lose you to this thing . . . if I have to watch it take you the way it's taking him . . . I won't survive it. You are the only thing in life that truly matters to me."

She turned her cheek into his palm, closed her eyes, and let the tears come. "And if we leave him to die alone in some boarding-house room because we were afraid? What kind of people does that make us? What kind of story do we tell our children one day—if God spares us to have them?"

Karl pulled her against him then, hard, like he could shield her from

11

the future itself. She buried her face in his shirt and breathed him in—woodsmoke, coffee, the faint lye-soap smell of the life they'd built together.

He rested his chin on the top of her head. "I'm not brave enough to choose between you and him," he said, voice muffled in her hair. "God help me, I'm not."

Keri's arms tightened around his waist. "Then we don't choose," she whispered. "We choose both. We bring him home. We give him our bed, the south room with the good light, every egg and every drop of milk the cow will give. We burn sage and carbolic, and we open the windows even when it's freezing. And every night we thank God for one more day that it hasn't come for us yet."

She pulled back just far enough to look up at him. "And if—if—the worst comes, we face it together. I'd rather have ten years with you and know we did right by your father than fifty years looking away from what love asked of us."

Karl's eyes searched hers for a long, long time. At last, he bent and pressed his forehead to hers.

"I love you so much it scares me worse than consumption ever could," he said hoarsely.

"I know," she answered, tears sliding down to where their skin touched. "I'm terrified too. But I love you more than I'm afraid."

He kissed her then—slow, deliberate, like a vow renewed in the dark kitchen of a little Dakota house that might soon hold death itself. When they parted, he kept one of her hands clasped between both of his.

"First light tomorrow," he said, "we'll take the train. Red can handle things here for a couple of weeks. We'll sell the ranch, settle the stock, and bank whatever might be salvaged. Then we bring Pa home."

Keri nodded, squeezing his hand until her knuckles went white. "Together," she said.

"Together," he echoed. "All the way to the end—his, or ours."

Keri swallowed hard, her mind racing. Train fare wasn't cheap, and their savings were thin—barely enough for the seed and new plow they'd need come spring. But they had little choice. She couldn't bear the thought of sending Karl on such an errand on his own. That would be too much of a strain on both of them. They had to find a way to make the long, rattling journey. It could take a month by the time they arrived there, settled whatever needed to be done, and returned home. Someone would have to help tend to the horses and homestead while they were gone. She captured Karl's numb gaze.

"The train leaves here at daylight?" Karl's eyes focused on her as their thoughts melded.

"Yes." His voice was barely a whisper, but his expression spoke endless words—fear, pain, determination. "We have a bit of cash. Enough, I think, to pay the fare."

Keri grimaced. "I shouldn't have bought supplies this morning." Karl gathered her in his arms again, pressing her close. She sensed the trembling anxiety in his heart.

"No. You did right. Red's going to need to eat while we're gone." He held Keri away from himself for a moment, a familiar twinkle in his eyes. "You know how Red can eat!" His attempt at lightening the moment was like a balm to Keri's nervous tension, even if it was a thin veil over Karl's own concerns.

He pulled a chair away from the table and sat, the letter's weight still heavy between them. Keri turned back to the stove, ladling beans into bowls, the noontime routine grounding her even as her thoughts spun toward Wyoming and the uncertain days ahead. Gran's plea echoed in her mind: Come quick as you're able.

The dim glow of the smoldering wick in the oil lamp lingered like a reluctant ghost, casting faint, flickering shadows across the modest second-floor bedroom. Karl had snuffed it out with a practiced twist of his fingers just moments before, but the ember clung stubbornly to life, its acrid tang of kerosene weaving through the cool night air.

Since Gran's departure three weeks ago, Keri had felt the house was too empty, too quiet. The gloomy pall brought on this morning by her letter mimicked the smoldering wick, refusing to dissipate. The sturdy wooden bed frame, covered with a straw mattress draped in faded linens, seemed especially unyielding to Keri tonight. As she gazed around the room, the chipped porcelain basin, still damp from evening use, gleamed in the moonlight atop a scarred washstand in the corner. The single window, framed by Gran's hand sewn lacy curtains, allowed the fading summer's evening breeze to stir the delicate fabric with what appeared to be hesitant breaths. Moonlight began pouring through the warped window glass in silvery rivulets, gilding the rough-hewn plank floor and coaxing dust motes into a lazy, ethereal waltz.

13

Keri lay on her side, her body curled toward the empty expanse of the room, eyes wide and unblinking as they adjusted to the growing darkness. The mattress dipped and creaked softly beneath their combined weight, the feathers in her pillow sighing with each shallow, uneven breath she drew. It had been two months since their wedding—a dizzying blur of struggle and answered prayer under Dakota sunsets, heartfelt vows spoken to one another and the world, and the quiet thrill of building a life from the raw clay of the frontier. But tonight, for the first time, an invisible wall had risen between them, thick and unyielding as the late August evening chill that would soon begin to seep through the chinks in the walls. She felt it in the rigid line of Karl's body beside her, in the jagged rhythm of his sighs that mocked the steady cadence of sleep. His arm, which had so often draped over her waist like a shield against the world's uncertainties, now lay stiff at his side, fingers twitching sporadically as if wrestling phantoms in the dark.

Her heart twisted with a frustration laced with tenderness, a familiar ache blooming in her chest like an old bruise pressed too hard. It echoed the relentless pain that had shadowed her just months earlier, dredging up ghosts of loss: the sudden, shattering void left by the massive spring flood, her father's shocking heart attack, the way the world had tilted on its axis as everything familiar fell away, leaving her adrift in grief's unforgiving current. For the past months, joy had pushed the memories of her battles to the back of her mind until now. Gran's letter, tucked away in the drawer of the washstand like a sealed indictment, had reopened suppressed but unhealed wounds. Gran's words painted a portrait of Alex—fading like a spent candle, his once-robust frame hollowed by illness and despair. Keri was all too familiar with the loss of a father. Her heart ached to bring Karl some comfort and assurance.

"Oh, Papa," she thought, the words a silent sob in her mind as tears brimmed at the edges of her eyes. "How can losing you still be so painful? Did you know, in those final, labored breaths, how I'd ache to see you just one more time, to hear the sound of your voice again? God, is this the shadow Karl carries now—the gnawing uncertainty, the dread of doors closing forever? I need to hear from you, to find words I can share to encourage hope and trust."

Her plea seemed to merge silently with the blackness of the night as a deep sense of helplessness washed over her for the first time in a while. It was a tide she knew too well, pulling at the edges of her resolve. Karl's mind

14

appeared to churn like a thunderhead she couldn't pierce, and small wonder. From the sounds of Gran's letter, the ranch near Laramie was unraveling thread by thread. Last winter's blizzards had been merciless, scouring the Laramie Plains like a divine scourge, claiming more than half the Richmond herd in drifts of snow and starvation. Selling the land—three generations of blood and sweat poured into its sunbaked soil—seemed the only path left, a bitter pill no one ever wanted to swallow. Their hasty supper of cornbread and strong coffee, eaten in weighty, uncomfortable silence, now sat like a stone in her gut.

"You have to sleep," Keri chided herself, even as her own tension coiled tighter, a spring wound to breaking. Dawn was mere hours away, and with it would come the rumble of the train at Yankton's depot. Their journey westward—a grueling 700 or more miles through the heart of the frontier—loomed like a gaunt specter. Karl knew the journey well, having traveled back and forth to the ranch when Alex first fell ill.

First, a short haul south to Sioux City, Iowa, where the Missouri's muddy waters would give way to the endless Nebraska prairies. Then, the Union Pacific's Overland Route would carry them onward: through wind-whipped grasslands dotted with buffalo remnants and sod-house homesteads, into the jagged embrace of the Rockies, where echoes of the 1880s cattle boom still lingered in tales of vast herds thundering across open ranges. Stops for coal and water, delays from the looming autumn rains or stray longhorns fouling the tracks, could stretch the trip to thirty hours or more—a test of endurance in cramped cars that Karl described as "thick with the scents of tobacco and unwashed travelers."

For Keri, the idea of the trip was daunting enough: leaving behind the fragile sanctuary of their homestead, the mares in the corral, the garden plot in its last throes with valuable gleanings of harvest. But for Karl, the trek seemed far more than one more voyage; he seemed to view it as a reckoning, a coming to terms with both his past and his future.

She turned her head on the pillow, the linen cool against her cheek, and studied his profile etched in moonlight. His jaw clenched like weathered oak, eyes locked on the ceiling beams as if he might find some mysterious comfort in the dark whorls of grain. The strong confidence and strength that Keri had come to know so well in her young husband were absent as vulnerability stripped Karl bare. She understood that the anxiety of reaching his father warred with the terror of what he'd find, and that the sale of

15

the ranch and bringing Alex to the homestead might disrupt the peace and contentment she and Karl had enjoyed since their wedding. Clearly, the illness's cruel advance had taken a terrible grip on Alex after a cascade of blows—the winter's toll on the cattle, the gut-wrenching loss of Jamie, and then Karl's departure, heeding what he'd sworn was God's summons to preach the Gospel amid Dakota's sod churches and settler souls. The thought had crossed her mind, too, that Karl's decision to leave the ranch had acted like a final nail in a proverbial coffin for his father.

The silence between Keri and Karl stretched taut as a bowstring until Keri could bear it no longer. She shifted closer to Karl, the hem of her nightgown whispering against his chambray shirt. She prayed, as she gathered her thoughts, that somehow, she could bring some relief to Karl's pain.

"Karl . . . is there anything I can do? Anything at all?" Keri whispered.

In the velvet dark, his hand sought hers, fingers lacing together in a grip that trembled with unspoken pleas. His touch was warm, roughened by years of reins and fence-mending, a map of the life he would soon trade for the pulpit and preaching.

"Pray with me, Keri," he murmured, voice gravel-rough with the strain of held-back tears. "Mine . . . they feel like they're bouncing off the clouds tonight. I want to trust God, but doubt keeps dragging me under. It feels like some unseen force is sweeping away my pleas—nothing echoes back but the wind."

They lay entwined in the hush, the distant yip of coyotes a mournful counterpoint to the crickets' chorus around them. Minutes bled into an eternity before Karl's words broke loose again. He spoke haltingly, as though each word cost him dearly.

"There's more, Keri. Things that have been churning over and over in my thoughts, now." He drew a ragged breath. "Pa's illness . . . it's not going to get better. Someone will have to sit with him day and night before long—watch him cough his life away, wipe droplets of blood from his lips, do what's possible to keep his fever down. That someone will be me, you, and Gran. We can try to keep Alex in. His room, open the windows, burn sulfur, do everything the doctors say . . . but the truth is, once he's under our roof, the sickness will be in the house with us."

Ker's heart thudded against her ribs, yet she said nothing, only pressed his hand to let him know he should go on.

Karl's voice dropped even lower. "Folks won't come calling. Not neighbors, not the ladies from church with their baskets and good intentions. They'll likely be kind from a distance, but they'll probably keep their children at home. We'll have to ask Red—plain-out ask him—if he's willing to risk stepping inside our door anymore, or if he'd rather meet me in the barn, take his meals there. And the church . . ." A tremulous confusion permeated his words. "What will they say when their new preacher lives in a consumptive house? Will they still want me laying hands on their babies for blessing, shaking hands after service, breathing the same air while I preach? Some will call our gesture heroic. Many will call it reckless. Foolish. A danger to the whole congregation, even the community."

He turned his face toward her, the darkness hiding the struggle visible in his eyes. "I have to hear from God, Keri. Plain and clear. Because right now every fear sounds louder than his voice, and I'm terrified that I'm about to drag you—maybe this whole community—into something we can't come back from."

The weight of his words settled over her like a sodden blanket. She felt the same chill he did; the same images flashed behind her eyes—empty pews, averted faces, Red hesitating on the porch, hat in hand. Yet deeper still, beneath the fear, something steadier stirred.

She found his cheek with her palm. "Karl . . . I have my reservations, too. I won't lie about it. I think, too, of the terrible consequences of your Pa's illness. Long nights, giving up so many things we have enjoyed these past months. Being separated from church members and wondering if anyone will feel safe in our presence again." Her voice cracked, then steadied. "But then I hear something else. The same quiet voice that told me—clear as morning—that it was okay to love a man I barely knew and follow him as he answers God's call on his life. That voice is telling me now: bring Alex home. Trust me."

Karl was silent so long she felt tears gathering in her own eyes.

"I want to hear that voice, too," he whispered at last. "Lord knows I do." Then, as a levee crumbles under floodwaters, another confession surged forth. "I'm thinking I shouldn't have left the ranch when I did. Pa was reeling—James gone, the herd decimated, snowdrifts burying our future . . ."

"That ranch . . . it was Pa's legacy," Karl continued. "Grandpa scratched it from the dirt with nothing but grit and prayer. Pa poured his soul into it

17

after his dad passed, built it into something proud. He always figured I'd take the reins one day, preserve the family operation. If I'd stayed, just a season longer . . . maybe I could've helped pick up the pieces and then come to Dakota with a clear heart. Maybe he wouldn't be fading like this, bit by bit."

Keri's breath snagged, a sharp intake that bordered on a gasp. She bolted upright, the quilts pooling around her waist like spilled milk, and fixed her gaze on his shadowed form. Moonlight caught the shimmer of tears welling in her eyes, turning them to quicksilver. "But that would mean—" The words died on her tongue, almost too brutal to voice. "We would never meet . . . never . . . marry." She forced herself to voice the words, then paused to gauge Karl's response. The implication of his thoughts stabbed deep, threatening to unravel the delicate weave of their union.

Karl rose beside her, the bed frame protesting with a low, mournful creak, and drew her into his arms. She melted against him, cheek pressed to the steady thunder of his heart, his chin resting atop her tousled hair. "I'm sorry," he breathed into the crown of her head, regret lacing his words. "You're right as rain. I had to come—God surely planned it just that way." Now he paused, sighing deeply. "It's just . . . this guilt keeps whispering that Pa's breaking because of my leaving. He lost James, me, and Gran. All in a few weeks. It was all too much. I'm sure of it now. Why would God allow all these things to happen? What if it was the final blow that led to all this?"

Tears spilled hot down Keri's cheeks as his raw torment echoed her own fresh scars. His words echoed her own all-too-recent thoughts and fears. He and Gran had been her saving grace at a time when her world seemed to spin out of control. The last thing she wanted to think was that her deliverance had initiated such a painful existence for Alex or for Karl. Gently, she eased back, cradling his face in her palms, thumbs tracing the salt-and-pepper stubble, the fevered warmth of his skin.

"Remember, when I thought every hope was gone? That God had turned his back on me? But he sent you. He sent Gran. I will never believe that any of that was a coincidence. He had a plan for me, for us." Keri couldn't see Karl's face in the deepening night, but she felt a measure of peace come over him. "He hasn't abandoned your pa, either. What is that scripture about my grace is sufficient for you? None of us is facing this alone, Karl. I'm right beside you. Gran is with us. We're all there for your pa. As Gran's letter said, God is with all of us."

Karl drew her closer still, foreheads touching like halves of a whole, breaths intermingling in the sacred quiet. "Grace," Karl echoed, the word a balm, soft as morning mist. "My grace is sufficient for you, my power is made perfect in weakness. Second Corinthians, 12:9." Karl leaned across the divide, his lips brushing her cheek in a kiss feather-light as grace itself. "No wonder God brought us together, Keri Richmond. You're the blessing I didn't even know I needed."

At last, the wick's ember surrendered with a final, defiant sputter, plunging the room into profounder shadow. Yet in that velvet blind, the wall between them began to crumble, tension uncoiling like a fist unclenching.

"We must try to rest," Keri murmured, her voice a gentle prod. "There's little chance we'll sleep very well on that train. Red's due at first light—I want flapjacks and hot black coffee for him. Without him, I'd be forced to stay home."

Karl nodded in agreement, further dispelling the gloom that had held him moments ago. "You're right. Pray Gran is the voice that sways Pa. Since Ma slipped away . . ." Karl's words trailed as a long-remembered grief resurfaced. "She was ill for all of two years before she passed. Doctors had no idea what truly ailed her. Pa . . . he couldn't face it at first. He almost acted like her frailty was a choice, a stubbornness he could will away. Wouldn't even speak her name after she passed. Now, with you beside me, I understand that better. Pa's known a lot of grief in his life."

Keri's fingers tightened around his, a vow in the gesture. "I know that shadow of loss too well," she whispered, then bowed her head, drawing him into the circle of their joined hands. "But now I know where to turn for help." She grasped both Karl's hands and bowed her head. "Lord, we need you so right now. Alex needs your touch for healing, but mostly for peace. Quiet these storms in our hearts, grant us sleep as a mercy. We trust you're protecting us during our travels and, above all, that you're even now providing the patience we need to walk this new path."

The prayer hung like incense in the room, simple and fervent. The night beyond the window deepened, stars twinkling overhead like promises etched in ink. In the hush of their chamber, grace held sway, a quiet dawn breaking within. With one last embrace, Keri and Karl settled into the bed as their eyelids finally grew heavy with sleep.

At last, the wick's ember surrendered with a final, defiant sputter, plunging the room into profounder shadow. Yet in that velvet blind, the wall between them began to crumble, tension uncoiling like an unclenching fist.

CHAPTER TWO

Held in His Hand

The first pale light of dawn crept across the yard as the wagon Red drove rattled to a stop beside the porch. Steam still rose from the coffee pot on the stove inside, and the scent of flapjacks lingered in the crisp air. Karl stepped out first, valise in one hand, the other reaching to steady Keri as she followed with her smaller carpetbag. Their tickets were already tucked inside Karl's coat pocket, the train due in less than an hour.

Red swung down from the wagon seat, then turned to Karl with the easy grin that usually greeted every morning. "Thanks again for that breakfast. It might well keep me. Till you get back." But Karl did not return Red's smile. He set the valise down, squared his shoulders, and spoke before the moment could pass.

"Red . . . there's something I've got to ask you straight out, man to man." Karl's voice was low, almost lost beneath the jingle of trace chains as the horses shifted. "Once Pa's here . . . once the consumption is in the house . . . you'll be welcome any time, same as always. But I won't blame you one bit if you'd rather keep clear of the doorstep. Folks say it's catching. I have to know—are you comfortable coming inside after he arrives, or would you rather meet me at the barn or out in the corrals?"

The yard went still. Even the horses seemed to listen.

Red studied Karl for a long, quiet moment. Then he reached out and laid a weathered hand on Karl's shoulder, the grip firm, steady, the way a man steadies a skittish colt.

"Son," Red began, voice rough with memory, "some fifteen years ago I opened this very door to three strangers headed west—whole family burning up with scarlet fever. I had a wife then, pretty as spring columbine, a son and two little girls with curls just like their mama's. I took those travelers in because it was the only Christian thing to do. A month later I buried my wife and all three babies in the same week." His eyes glistened, but his gaze

21

never wavered. "It was the hardest thing I ever walked through, Karl, and likely the hardest I ever will. Some nights I still hear their voices on the wind."

Karl's throat worked; he could find no words.

Red squeezed his shoulder tighter. "But if the Lord put those same travelers on my porch tomorrow, I'd open the door again. Because it was right. Helping the suffering—especially family—that's what we're here for. Sometimes love costs dear. I pray to God it won't cost you and Keri what it cost me. But your pa? He'll be welcomed here as a brother, as a precious child of the King. I'll sit at his bedside if need be, read him Scripture, hold the basin when he coughs—whatever's required. We're all in this together, Karl. Every step."

Karl's eyes filled so quickly he couldn't blink the tears away. One slipped down his cheek and caught in the stubble he hadn't taken time to shave. Without a word he pulled Red into a fierce embrace, the kind two men seldom allow themselves on an ordinary morning. Red clapped him hard on the back, once, twice, then held on just as tightly.

"You're a gem, Red," Karl managed at last, voice breaking. "A rare gem. We'll need every bit of help the Lord sends, and knowing you're standing with us . . . that means more than I can ever say."

Red gave a gruff laugh that sounded suspiciously wet. "Aw now, none of that. You'll have me blubbering before the sun's fairly up." He stepped back, swiped the heel of his hand across his eyes, and jerked a thumb toward the wagon. "Come on, you two. Train won't wait, and I've got a preacher and his bride to deliver safe to the depot."

Keri, who had watched the whole exchange with tears shining on her own lashes, reached out and pressed Red's arm as she passed. No words were needed; the gratitude in her eyes said everything.

As Karl lifted Keri onto the wagon seat, the first golden edge of sunrise broke over the hills, painting the three of them in light warm as mercy itself.

The dew-kissed platform at Yankton's depot bustled with activity just moments after dawn. The sky hung like a vast, unspooled bolt of purplish-blue velvet, twinkling with the fading silver brilliance of late stars that winked reluctant farewells as the rising sun coaxed the veil of night to slip away. No moon lingered to soften the edges of the breaking day; instead, a thin veil of high-altitude clouds streaked the eastern horizon in wispy grays.

The air bit lightly at travelers with the promise of soon-coming frost and carried the faint, briny tang of the Missouri River just beyond the tracks. Overhead, the dome of heaven felt infinite, pressing down with a hush that amplified the distant huff of the locomotive gathering steam. The first blush of rose-tinted light bled upward from the unseen sun, casting the depot's lanterns in a warmer, almost apologetic glow. Keri pulled her shawl tighter while Karl's strong arm guided her steps toward the train.

The Dakota Southern Railway's black iron flanks gleamed faintly under oil lamps as it slowly lurched forward with a resonant whistle that sliced the early morning quiet, pulling them southeast along the serpentine curve of the Missouri's south bank. What remained of Yankton's modest clapboard homes and buildings after the massive April flood and the silhouette of the territorial capital's white-domed building receded swiftly, swallowed by the soon-enveloping embrace of the Loess Hills. The ancient, wind-sculpted bluffs rose in gentle swells of tawny earth, their slopes cloaked in a patchwork of the encroaching fall's palette. Goldenrod-yellow grasses nodded in the breeze, laced with the rust-red spines of sumac and the stubborn green of bur oak thickets that clung to the hillside crests. Dawn's light, now a soft peach suffusion, gilded the river's lazy meanders, which were visible through the car's fogged panes. The Big Muddy, as the rivermen called it, uncoiled like a slumbering serpent, its chocolate-brown waters flecked with patches of multi-colored leaves at the eddies. Cottonwood groves fringed the river where an amber confetti shower of leaves would soon dot the landscape.

The rhythmic clatter of the train wheels against the tracks filled the cramped passenger car, a monotonous soundtrack to the vast plains blurring past the window. Karl silently stared out at the endless horizon, his hands clasped tightly in his lap, knuckles white. Beside him, Keri shifted in her seat, the sparsely padded wooden bench already inflexible against her slight frame. Her gaze flicked between the landscape flowing past her sight and her husband's tense profile. There had been little time for conversation this morning as they scurried to gather their bags and provide final instructions for Red. While Red's heartfelt confirmation of their plan to bring Alex to the homestead took the edge off the morning chill, shadows of doubt persisted.

Now, as the train raced across the plains, everything within Keri wanted to hear again Karl's reassuring words of confidence as they began this journey into the unknown. But they sat statue-like, shoulder to shoulder

23

on the hard bench. Karl wore the dark-gray wool coat gifted to him back in Wyoming after he announced his commitment to becoming a pastor. It was a second-hand item, once black but softened by sun and prairie wind. The hem brushed the tops of his boots; the collar stood high and close, fastened with a plain bone button. A faint patch at the left elbow (Keri's neat darning) was the only obvious sign of wear.

In the slight chill of this early late August morning, the coat was more than ample protection. However, if their instincts proved true, and their return came well into September, the coat would be necessary. The white cotton carefully starched shirt underneath the coat was already faintly creased from the morning's bustle. The turned-down collar was secured by a narrow black silk neckband tied in a bow at the throat. Even without the common pastor's garb, Karl's countenance and demeanor would have easily revealed his godly heart. It was one of the numerous characteristics that had won over Keri's heart. Inwardly, she smiled as she realized that even in his best dress—square-toed, well-oiled leather boots, scuffed at the toes from homestead chores, and low-crowned, wide-brimmed black felt hat—he carried the ghost of barn horses, barn dust, and chores.

His Bible—black leather, edges rubbed soft—rested atop a small canvas valise on his lap. Hearing his quiet and certain voice would affirm the words her own heart kept rehearsing: God is in this. I am not afraid. She needed to borrow from Karl's peace again, the way she had so often done in months past. But the train car was filled with equally uneasy passengers, who exchanged few glances and kept their gaze either on their own small space or the blurred landscape visible through the soot-streaked windows. Unease would not be dismissed.

Keri's gaze settled on a salesman sitting across the aisle, wearing a loud plaid formless suit that hung straight on his boxy frame like a flour sack. The jacket's brass buttons gleamed, and a sample case of patent medicines was wedged between his knees. His bowler hat tilted rakishly; a gold watch chain looped across a waistcoat strained by too many hotel dinners. He hummed a tune Keri couldn't identify and offered those around him peppermints from a tin. In the uncomfortable silence between the passengers, as the salesman unwrapped another peppermint, the crackle was loud as gunfire. A young mother nearby hushed her startled toddler with a crust of bread.

Behind Karl, two farmers argued over crop prices in low, rumbling tones. In homespun shirts and suspenders, the two shared a newspaper,

24

their calloused thumbs leaving prints on the margins. One wore a wide-brimmed felt hat pushed back on a sun-bleached forehead; the other's wool cap emitted a faint odor of a livestock filled barn. Their boots—caked with barnyard earth—rested on a burlap sack of seed corn.

At the far end of the car, tucked into the very last seat as though she wished to disappear between the pages of her book, sat a spinster schoolteacher whose entire bearing declared that the world had already taken its measure of her and found her wanting, yet she refused to yield an inch.

She was perhaps forty-five, though sorrow and plain living had carved the marks of sixty. Her dress was a severe black alpaca, high-necked and long-sleeved even in the close warmth of the car. Its fabric was worn to a muted sheen at the elbows and cuffs, every tuck and seam as straight and unyielding as the rules she no doubt drilled into her pupils. A single jet brooch, the size of a nickel and just as cold, fastened the collar that circled her thin neck like a parson's noose. Her iron-gray hair was drawn back so tightly that it pulled the corners of her eyes into a perpetual expression of mild disapproval, then twisted into a knot so small and hard it might have been hammered there by years of discipline.

Pinched-nose spectacles, the lenses small ovals of inexpensive glass, perched on a nose sharp enough to mark examination papers without a pencil. Each time the train lurched or the wheels screamed around a curve, those lenses caught the morning light streaming through the smudged window and flung it back in tiny, disapproving flashes. Her lips, thin and bloodless, moved silently over the words of Little Women as if she were hearing the March girls for the first time and quietly correcting their grammar even as she read.

From her left wrist hung a drawstring purse so small and delicately made it might once have belonged to a child; black silk, faded almost gray, with a few glass beads left where others had long since fallen away. It held, one suspected, little more than a handkerchief edged in tired lace, a few coins for coffee at the next station, and the return half of a third-class ticket that would carry her home again to empty rooms and the echoing schoolhouse bell.

She never looked up, not once, though she surely felt the curious glances of the newlyweds midway down the car. It was easy to imagine she had trained herself long ago to expect nothing from the world except the next page, the next lesson, the next lonely evening by a single lamp, and she

25

intended to go on meeting that expectation with impeccable posture and an unbreakable silence.

Beside the stove, a lean-framed soldier, skin etched with the prairie sun's merciless tally and eyes squinting perpetually against the glare of the prairie sun, sat resolutely, gazing out the window. His sky-blue uniform clung to him like a second skin, worn threadbare by days and months of service. His dark blue woolen shortcoat, reserved for mounted men, featured frayed hems—likely from encounters with brush and burrs—was adorned with yellow piping indicative of cavalry. His light blue trousers were tucked into black leather boots cracked from Dakota's freeze-thaw seasonal changes. Atop his head rode the typical wide crease-brimmed and tall crowned Stetson, adorned with a gold cord and insignia to signify his unit. A tin cup balanced on his knee, and his knapsack bore a faded regimental patch. Every so often, he muttered to himself.

The air carried the mingled scents of coal smoke, camphor, peppermint, and warm wool. Outside, telegraph wires flashed by like stitches in the sky, binding the wide prairie to the world Keri and Karl were quickly leaving behind.

Keri's throat tightened. She turned her face to the window, pretending to watch the landscape slide away, but she was really praying fiercely that Karl would sense the ache beside him. Part of her felt foolish, like a child who needed parental comfort. Still, this trip may change every expectation she had held for her life with Karl and their life on the homestead, which God had miraculously placed in their hands. It had all seemed so perfect, so fitting. Now, the uncertainty she had dreaded and sought to escape just a few months ago loomed again on the not-so-distant horizon.

Keri shifted again on the hard plush seat, the train's rhythmic clacking doing nothing to soothe the restlessness that coiled inside her. She smoothed the skirt of her traveling dress for the tenth time, though not a wrinkle dared show itself, and tried to fix her gaze on the Dakota prairie sliding past the window—endless waves of sun-bleached grass bending under a wind she could not feel. But the view blurred; tomorrow crowded in and would not be pushed aside.

Tomorrow she would meet Alex Richmond.

Karl sat beside her, hat on his knee, eyes half-closed in what might have looked like sleep to anyone else, but she knew better. His hand rested on hers, warm and steady, yet even that familiar weight could not quiet the questions that circled like hawks.

In the brief weeks since their wedding, she and Karl had forged something fierce and tender, a oneness she had never dreamed possible. They had prayed together in the quiet of dawn, laughed over burned biscuits, wept over letters from Wyoming, and fallen asleep night after night with whispered scripture on their lips, and arms entwined as though God Himself had knit them together while they slept. She carried the certainty of Karl's love like a secret flame against her heart.

But Alex had carried Karl first. Twenty years of first steps, first ponies, first heartbreaks, first prayers over scraped knees and dying calves. Alex had taught Karl to rope and ride and read, had stood silent beside open graves when Karl's mother and James were taken, had carved the ranch dream with calloused hands and a voice rough from wind and grief. Those bonds ran deeper than sentiment; they were carved into Karl's bones.

And what was she? A bride of mere weeks, a girl from Indiana who had never branded a calf or buried a child, who still flinched at the vastness of this western sky. What if Alex looked at her and saw only the outsider who had lured his only son away? What if the fever and the laudanum and the slow drowning of consumption had left him bitter, suspicious, stripped of every gentleness Karl remembered? What if he blamed her for Karl's absence when his world was collapsing around him? What if, in some dark corner of his wasting mind, he believed she had stolen what little family he had left?

She had never heard Alex's voice except through Karl's recounting— sometimes fond, sometimes edged with pain. She did not know if he would greet her with courtesy or coldness, with gratitude or resentment. She did not know if he would see Christ in her willingness to open their home, or only recklessness in bringing death itself under their roof.

Gran hadn't minced any words in her letter. Alex was deeply caught up in despair. I must commit to praying about the pain plaguing Alex. She closed her eyes for a moment, fixing her thoughts on Alex and his need for peace and healing. Cause him to turn to you, Lord." She lifted her silent plea, then continued her fervent prayer. Heal whatever is breaking his heart and his spirit. Please protect Karl from discouragement and guide my thoughts according to your will and purpose for all the changes that seem to be coming.

Karl's fingers tightened briefly over hers, as though he felt the tremor

27

she tried to hide. She glanced at him; his eyes were open now, soft with understanding.

"You're worrying again," he murmured, low enough that the other passengers would not hear. She gave the smallest nod, undone at how easily he read her.

He leaned close, his breath warm against her ear. "Pa's going to love you, Keri. Because I do. And because you're the answer to prayers he stopped daring to pray a long time ago."

She wanted to believe him. With all her heart she wanted to believe him. But the train hurtled on toward Wyoming, and tomorrow waited at the end of the line like a door she was not sure she was brave enough to open.

Karl's hands were maps of lifelong hours of labor. The heel of his right hand carried a permanent crescent scar where a panicked yearling once jerked at the halter and tore the skin to the bone. Over his knuckles, the skin was shiny, stretched from countless mornings spent wrestling bridle and harness buckles in the cold. Without looking her way, he squeezed her hand once, firm and deliberate. I am here. I am not afraid.

She risked a glance. His eyes were on the horizon, but his thumb traced a small circle on the back of her hand. Trust me. Trust Him.

Her breath caught, half sob, half laugh. Her lack of self-control and confidence distressed her. Lord, I want to be strong for Karl, but my heart is a storm. Quiet the fear that keeps taking over my thoughts. She pressed her lips together to mask the depth of her emotion. The train rattled on, an iron heartbeat beneath them.

The salesman offered his tin; Karl shook his head politely. The toddler dropped a wooden soldier; it rolled under Keri's boot. She bent to retrieve it, and when she straightened, she noted that the corners of Karl's mouth were pulled down in a way that wasn't quite a frown, more a quiet surrender to the uncertainty inside. His gaze shifted from her to the prairie where endless grasses were painted with warm shades of gold, red, and fading greens under a paling August sky. The press of the unknown had done its slow work on Karl's face—furrows at his brow, mouth held grim, eyes fixed on a horizon that offered no answers.

Keri forced herself to relax back onto the wooden seat, resolving herself to accept that, no matter what tomorrow brought, God was in it. Even though the impending battle loomed over them like a storm cloud, they were not in it alone. Grace. God says grace is sufficient. She could almost hear Gran's voice repeating the words. Gran's comforting presence would be so welcome when she met them at the Laramie depot, her unfailing wisdom a welcome reprieve from the oppressive thoughts plaguing both of them now. Perhaps she would pack a bit of food, too. The sparse number of biscuits, corn bread, and coffee beans Keri had hastily managed to pack into a flour sack would barely carry them through the next 24 hours. At one dollar per cup, the thought of purchasing coffee on the train was completely impractical.

After squeezing her eyes shut tight for one more moment in an effort to will away her angst, Keri untied the drawstring that secured the small bag on her lap and grasped the diary and pencil within. Just the touch of the diary against her hand brought a measure of peace as it brought Red to mind. He had so thoughtfully gifted it to her on her 18th birthday this past May. It now held treasured thoughts of her healing journey after the destruction of the disastrous floodwaters and loss of her father, as well as her growing relationship with Karl and Gran. Slipping it out of the bag, she carefully opened the leather covers to review its contents. The early morning sun cast comforting golden rays across the pages.

The first page was dated May 12, 1881, her own girlish script dancing across the lines.

" *May 20, 1881*

Eighteen today.

Gran says I am a woman now, but the mirror still shows the same freckled girl who used to chase grasshoppers across the pasture with Pa laughing behind me. Only the laughter is gone, and the south pasture belongs to strangers.

It was a happy day and a sorrowful one, all intertwined so tightly I could not tell which strand hurt most. I kept expecting Pa to come through the kitchen door, his sweat-soaked shirt evidence of another hard day's work, teasing me about being old enough to vote if only the territory thought women had sense. Instead there was only the wind rattling the windowpane and the ache that has taken up permanent residence under my ribs.

Gran must have seen it in my eyes, because she pulled me close and whispered, "Today we choose joy, child. Your pa would insist on it." Then she brought out the gift she had tucked away in her dresser: a dress the color of midnight sky just before the stars come out. Royal blue, rich as

29

anything I've ever owned, with a full row of tiny fabric-covered buttons marching down the front like soldiers. When I slipped it over my head the fabric felt like water, cool and alive, and for the first time in weeks I didn't feel like a homeless waif.

I twirled in the kitchen until Gran and Red laughed aloud, until the skirt belled out around me and the buttons caught the lamplight and threw it back in little blue sparks. Red clapped like I was on a circus stage, and Gran's eyes shone wet and proud. In that moment, wearing a color bright enough to shame the prairie sky, I dared to believe I might have a future after all. Something that belongs only to me and to whatever God still has planned.

And Karl . . .

I cannot even write his name without my heart doing that foolish skip it has learned lately. He stood in the doorway longer than necessary, hat in his hands, staring as though he had never seen a girl in a blue dress before. He didn't say a word, but there was a look in his eyes I hadn't seen before.

I have never been beautiful, not truly, but tonight I felt it. With the dress, I suppose I felt eighteen.

Lord willing, there will be many more pages in this journal. Red says a woman needs a place to keep her secrets and her dreams. I think he is right. Tonight my secret is simple and terrifying and bright as new buttons: I am alive. And I am beginning to hope again.

Keri clearly recalled the intense, troubling attraction to Karl that the evening of her birthday had brought on. The ink expressing her thoughts had browned somewhat, but the memory rose fresh as a morning blossom. Keri's thumb traced the word, Karl. That evening, she could not have imagined how the depth of her connection and devotion to this man would grow. She could never have anticipated the intense suffering she experienced now as she identified with the pain in his heart.

The girl who wrote those lines just weeks ago had already grown and changed, in part thanks to this man God brought into her life. Now, it seemed God had more changes, potential for more growth in all the future held. The night she penned his name, Keri was unsettled about her attraction to Karl. Now she knew deep inside there was no reason to be distressed. Just a need to walk closely to God every moment of each day.

She pressed the diary to her breast. Thank You, Lord, she breathed, the prayer rising wordless and warm. You saw me twirling in that blue dress and knew the details of every day that has unfolded since. You gave me a man whose heart is dedicated to you. I will trust your word, patiently wait, and follow as you unfold all the details in the days ahead.

Across the aisle, the toddler dropped his soldier again; Karl bent to retrieve it without looking up from his own reading. His profile—strong, sun-lined, peaceful—was the same one that had held Keri's attention from the first moments they met. The train whistle moaned, but inside Keri a quieter song began: Delight yourself in the Lord . . . She smiled, small and fierce, and turned the page to write anew.

Karl let out a heavy sigh that was loud and clear even over the rattle of the train car. Keri's head snapped up, her pencil going limp in her hand as she turned all her attention on him. His lame smile did little to dissipate her concern. Her piercing gaze was unwavering as she waited for some indication of what instigated his melancholy: a fleeting shadow across his features, perhaps, or some whispered word about what was claiming his thoughts. He leaned close to her and whispered, "Keri, I . . . I feel like God is hiding from me. I can't understand it."

Karl glanced across the aisle to determine if their conversation was being overheard. Nothing indicated that any of the surrounding passengers were eavesdropping on the murmured words.

The train lurched around a bend, iron wheels screaming, and Karl was on his feet before Keri could draw breath. One moment he stood at the coach door, staring out at the black prairie; the next he had pushed through and vanished onto the open platform. The door banged shut behind him, leaving only the echo of wind and the startled glances of nearby passengers.

Outside the door, the narrow platform, no more than four feet wide and eight feet long, was framed by iron railings no higher than a man's waist. A low gate of scrollwork barred the gap to the next car, its latch stiff with soot and prairie dust. The floor was rough pine planking, warped and blackened by cinders. A single oil lantern hung from a bracket above the door, its glass cracked and yellowed, swinging wildly with every lurch of the train.

The platform rocked beneath Karl's boots, the whole car swaying like a cradle on a giant's knee. Coal smoke whipped past in stinging gusts, carrying sparks that glowed orange before dying against the gathering darkness. Beyond the railing, the landscape blurred: telegraph poles flicked by like pickets, the endless dark prairie swallowing the lantern's feeble reach.

Keri's heart slammed against her ribs. She began to rise, then forced

31

herself to sit down again. Karl's Bible was lying on the bench beside her, its worn leather cover closed. *Your grace is sufficient. We trust in you, Lord.* She folded her hands and forced herself to repeat her faith in God's instructions, doing all she could to focus on what God had already shown her and avoid fearful thoughts.

The whistle shrieked, the train lurched again, and Karl stepped back inside. He slid the door shut behind him, the click of the latch soft against the steady rumble of the train. The car was dim now, only a few oil lamps swaying overhead, and the other passengers had settled into quiet or sleep. Keri looked up from her lap, heart still knotted from the long half-hour she had spent watching that door.

He didn't speak right away as he slipped into his seat. He simply took his seat beside her again, removed his hat, and let out a breath that sounded as though it had been held for days. The sharp edges that had cut into his face all afternoon were gone—smoothed away like wind erases tracks in new snow. His eyes, when they met hers, were clear, almost wondering.

"Keri," he said, voice low and steady, "I've been a fool."

She started to protest, but he shook his head and took her hand.

"I stood out there hollering at God like a stubborn child—'Speak, Lord! Tell me plain! Are we really to take Pa in? Do we sell the ranch? How do we pay the debts? How do I preach grace when I'm scared to death about what tomorrow might bring?' Silence. Nothing but the wind and the wheels and the dark closing in. I was furious at Him for leaving me dangling."

He gave a small, rueful laugh.

"Then the strangest thing happened. I got quiet—really quiet—and I felt him ask me one question, gentle as a hand on my shoulder: 'Karl, who did I trust the ranch to the day you left Wyoming?' I opened my mouth to answer 'Pa,' but before the word came out I knew that wasn't true. The ranch was never Pa's to carry alone, and it sure isn't mine now. It's been the Lord's all along. Every blade of grass, every cow and calf, every dollar of debt—he's the real owner. Pa was only the steward, and a weary one at that. I've been trying to take the ledger back out of God's hands, as if he dropped it the day Gran and I boarded the eastbound train."

Karl turned her hand palm-up and traced a slow line across it with his thumb.

"Then He brought three pictures to my mind, one right after another, plain as daylight. First, he showed me Pa—not the sick man coughing

32

endlessly in that little room, but Pa thirty years younger, standing at Ma's grave with me clinging to his legs. He was broken that day, Keri—broken clean in two—and he kept going. But it wasn't Pa that brought us through. Pa may not know it—yet—but it was God. If God was faithful then, he's faithful now. Pa's body may be failing, but the God who held him up then—when Pa didn't even recognize it—is still holding him. And he'll hold us while we hold Pa."

A soft "O-o-o-h!" Escaped Keri's lips. Karl grasped her hands more tightly, shifting toward her more.

"Then God reminded me of the night I asked you to marry me. I had nothing to offer you but a preacher's uncertain wage and a heart full of Wyoming dust. We didn't even know if I would be well again. Yet you said yes without asking for a single guarantee. That was grace, Keri—pure, reckless grace. And the Lord whispered, 'That's how I want you to love your father. Not with a plan that protects you from loss, but with open hands and a heart that says yes before it knows the cost.'"

Keri squeezed her eyes closed and nodded, leaning against Karl's chest. His voice caught, and he had to clear his throat before he continued.

"He showed me the cross. Just that. Nothing fancy—just the rough wood and the blood and the Son crying out, 'Why have You forsaken Me?' Jesus went to the cross so that I—you—Pa—would never have to be forsaken. And then I understood: the silence that's been frustrating me isn't absence. It's trust. God's not ignoring me—he's already spoken everything I need in Jesus. The rest is just learning to live what he's already said."

Karl lifted her hand and pressed it over his heart, keeping his voice low but earnest.

"So here's what I know now, plain and simple. We bring Pa home and love him with everything we have, for as many days as God gives. If the disease takes us too, we'll know God has a purpose in it and meet the same place we'll meet Pa again—on the other side of the grave, where there's no more coughing or debt or goodbyes." Keri's eyes brightened as Karl went on.

"The ranch? If it has to be sold to pay what's owed, we'll sign the papers with gratitude that it served its purpose. If God wants it kept, he'll send the means—buyers, rain, miracle cattle, I don't know. But it's his ranch, not ours."

"I agree," she whispered.

33

"And grace. That's the only way any of it works. We'll walk this road the same way God has led us through all the challenges of the past—one obedient, grace-soaked step at a time, borrowing strength we don't have from the one who has it all."

He looked at her then, eyes shining but unafraid.

"I'm not confused anymore, Keri. I'm not frustrated. I'm just . . . held. And I've never felt more like a man in all my life."

The train whistle sounded far ahead, mournful and sweet in the gathering night, and Karl drew her close. Outside, the first stars appeared—small, fierce promises keeping watch over a world that belonged, every inch of it, to a God who had never once looked away.

CHAPTER THREE

Stewards of the Storm

The Wyoming sun was sinking lower in the sky, like a weary sentinel, casting long shadows across the endless expanse of prairie as the wagon rattled up the dusty trail toward the Richmond ranch. Keri clutched Karl's hand tightly, her fingers interlaced with his in a grip that spoke volumes of her swirling emotions—anticipation mingling with a tinge of trepidation. Her own experience with loss and uncertainty kept bubbling up as they drew closer to the ranch. She found herself constantly turning from the temptation to act out of fear and submit to despair regarding what may unfold in the next few hours.

The vast landscape stretched out around them like an infinite canvas, painted in hues of gold and sage green, dotted with scrubby sagebrush that whispered in the gentle breeze. In the distance, herds of cattle grazed indifferently, their lowing a faint underscore to the creak of the wagon wheels and the rhythmic clip-clop of the horses' hooves.

Gran, with her silver hair tucked neatly under a faded blue bonnet, drove the team with the practiced ease of someone who had spent a lifetime navigating these rugged paths. She chattered away, her voice a warm counterpoint to the silence that otherwise enveloped them. "Oh, you'd love the wildflowers that come with spring, Keri dear. They blanket the hills like a quilt from heaven itself. And the stars at night—why, they're so bright you could read scripture by them."

Although Gran's words were lighthearted and uplifting, an undercurrent of tension followed them like a determined fog. The aged woman glanced back at them occasionally, her eyes crinkling with a mix of affection and concern for the young couple.

Keri forced a smile, but her thoughts returned again and again to what she had imagined so many times during the train ride—arriving at the ranch that Karl had described with such fondness, meeting his father, stepping into

35

a new phase of their life together, one filled with promise but not without challenges. Now, as the buildings came into view, reality pressed in like the dry wind whipping across the plains. What should she say if Alex didn't welcome her? What if the shadows of loss that hung over this ranch proved too dark for any light to pierce? What if resolving all the issues surrounding the ranch required more than they could afford? What if . . .

Karl squeezed her hand reassuringly. He hadn't said much since Gran informed them that Alex was likely to confront them about the risk of getting sick. "It'll be alright, Gran," Karl said. "God has given us an answer, and no matter who or what challenges that, we stand with God."

Keri cleared her throat before tentatively asking, "Do you think he doesn't want us to be here?"

Gran's eyes widened as she quickly answered. "No, child. I believe that, behind that crusty shell he's hidin' in, he is thrilled to see both of you. But it's not likely that he'll let you know that. We'd best get started so we're home before sunset. This time of year, the afternoon heat is quickly swallowed up in the evenin' chill."

Along the way, Karl's hazel eyes were fixed on the horizon as if some unseen source was offering guidance in the bright afternoon light. Keri was so thankful for the spiritual breakthrough they'd shared on the train, where faith had reignited in their souls like a spark in dry tinder. But returning home meant Karl would be facing the flames of reality: a failing ranch, a dying father, and the ghosts of a family fractured by hardship.

"There she is," Gran announced, pointing ahead with a weathered hand. The ranch emerged from the haze—a cluster of weathered buildings that spoke of endurance against the elements. The sturdy two-story log house stood at the center, its chimney reaching tall against the twilight sky. Flanking it was a bunkhouse for the hired hands, now eerily quiet with most of the men long gone due to the ranch's dwindling cattle herd. A barn leaned slightly to one side, battered by years of relentless wind, its red paint faded to a dull rose. Empty corrals held only a few horses that nickered softly at their approach, and two cows that chewed their cud with bovine indifference.

"Home sweet home," Gran added with a sigh, "at least what's left of it."

Karl's jaw tightened visibly, the muscles flexing under his stubbled skin, but he managed a small smile for Gran's sake. "It's good to see it again," he murmured, though his voice carried a note of strain. "I can see Pa's not been able to keep things up lately."

"We still got Chester," Gran said. "He's been so faithful all these years. There's a few head of cattle he checks every day, and he does what he can to keep things hanging together. I have a feelin' he might consider buyin' when we're ready to sell."

"What does Pa say about selling?" Karl studied Gran's face.

"We haven't talked much on it," she said. "He has a hard time talkin' without coughin' and I thought it best to wait till you got here. He's got to know that's the only path left to us."

Karl thought for a moment before speaking. "Gran, is Pa angry that I left the ranch? That I'm not stepping in to take his place?"

Now Gran hesitated for a moment. "There may be somethin' of that in his thoughts," she said. "But, Karl, you can't let that sway you from what you know God is callin' you to do. If Chester ends up buyin' the place, maybe that's God blessin' him. If Alex wants to be mad, he'll have to be mad at God."

As the wagon pulled to a stop in front of the house, a tall figure emerged from the shadowed porch, leaning heavily on a cane. Alex Richmond stood with his shoulders hunched forward, his once-robust frame now wasted by the consumption that ravaged his lungs. One gnarled hand gripped the porch rail, the other wrapped tight around a rough-hewn cane. The man who had once swung down from a horse without touching the stirrups now looked as though the three steps to the ground might cost him everything. His shirt hung loose on a frame that had wasted away, and the skin of his face was drawn tight over sharp bones. When he saw them, he started forward, slow and deliberate, leaning heavily on the cane with every careful step. Keri's breath caught as they drew nearer, and she saw the gauntness of his face, etched with deep lines of physical pain. Dark circles under his eyes were so prominent that they were visible from a distance, giving him a hollowed-out, haunting look.

Karl hopped down from the wagon first, then turned to help Keri, his hands steady on her waist as he lifted her to the ground. His touch lingered protectively on her arm, a silent affirmation of solidarity as he guided her toward Alex. They had only taken a few steps when Alex stopped as if an invisible line had been drawn in the dirt, and held up his hand, signaling them to stop.

"You sure you know what you're walkin' into?" His voice was hoarse,

37

thinner than Karl remembered. "This house . . . I'm poison right now. You get too close, you breathe the same air too long, you could carry it home with you. You could even die. I don't want you blindsided."

Karl didn't hesitate. He closed the distance until only the cane separated them. "We know the risk, Pa. We talked it through for the last two days."

Alex's pale eyes narrowed. "Then why'd you come? You want to die?"

Karl reached out and took his father's free hand. The fingers were cold, trembling slightly. "Pa, I need you to hear this straight from me, not second-hand through Gran or anybody else."

Alex's eyes flick up, guarded.

"Keri and I didn't come all this way just because we felt obligated. We came because we love you. Plain and simple. You're my father, and nothin'—not sickness, not distance, not the hard words we've traded over the years—is gonna' change that."

He leaned closer to Alex.

"This thing you're fightin' . . . it's ugly and it's unfair, and I hate it for you. But you don't have to carry it by yourself anymore. Whatever you need—sittin' with you through the nights that feel endless, holdin' your hand when the medicine makes you shake, or just sittin' quiet when words run out—we're here for all of it. No, expecting you to be strong or grateful or anything, you're not right now. We just want to walk through this with you, same way you walked through the hard stuff with me when I was little and didn't know how bad the world could hurt."

Karl reached out and rested his hand on his father's thin forearm.

"You're not a burden, Pa. We love you too much to stay away. And we're trusting God to bring all of us through this."

For a long moment, Alex didn't move. Then, so faintly Karl almost misses it, the older man's hand turned over beneath his son's and gave the slightest pressure—one squeeze, barely there, but enough.

Alex gave a short, bitter sputter. "Hmpfh. God ain't done much for me."

Karl pulled his father into an embrace despite his father's cold detachment, careful, as if holding something that might break. Alex stayed rigid, arms at his sides, but he didn't pull away.

"I'm sorry you're goin' through this," Karl said quietly against the worn flannel of his father's shirt. "I don't have answers for why. I just know I can trust Him, even when things seem impossible."

For a long moment, the only sound was the wind moving through the

38

sparse stand of pine trees behind the house.

Then Gran's sharp voice cut between them like a kitchen knife through warm bread as she swept in between the two.

"Alexander, I've told you a dozen times—we're leavin' the outcome in God's hands and that's final." She slipped her arm through Alex's and, with surprising briskness, began guiding him back to the porch. "Besides, these young 'uns have been on the road since dawn, and my good hot meal is gettin' cold. You want to hash out theology, we got all weekend for it. Right now we're goin' inside and eatin' before I have to warm everything up again."

Alex glanced at her, then at Karl, then at Keri waiting quietly behind Karl. Noticing his glance, Karl drew Keri close to his side, saying, "Pa, this is my wife, Keri. She is just one of the amazing blessings God has brought into my life."

Alex's gaze lingered on Keri's face, touching on the plain gold band on her finger, then slid away. He opened his mouth; the wind took whatever sound might have come. Something flickered across Alex's face—resignation, maybe, or the ghost of surrender. He gave the slightest nod to Keri. Gran slipped her arm through his and started toward the steps. "Lean on me and that stick both now. Supper's waitin'."

Karl caught Keri's eye. She offered a small, steady smile, and together they followed their family into the house.

Keri's mind raced. Everything within her yearned to reach out, to embrace this broken man and offer some balm for the pain that emanated from him like heat from a red-hot stove. Since Gran's letter arrived at the homestead, a profound sense of empathy had filled Keri's heart—for this stranger ravaged by illness and loss, for the father Karl loved despite the distance between them. She prayed fervently, silently again, asking God to soften Alex's heart, to prepare the way for healing of body, soul, and mind.

Gran stepped next to Keri, grasping her elbow in a comforting gesture. As Keri glanced at Gran, her gaze was met with the peace and wisdom she had come to know and appreciate. Just Gran's presence renewed Keri's resolve.

The four of them stepped into the familiar kitchen, boots scuffing across the worn pine floor that had known three generations of Richmond feet. The brilliant rays of the soon-to-fade afternoon sun streamed through lace-curtained windows, warming the worn wooden floors and casting

39

a golden glow over the room. A cast-iron stove dominated one wall, its surface polished to a shine, and the air carried the inviting aroma of meat and vegetables.

The kitchen table, scarred from years of use, stood in the center, surrounded by mismatched chairs that spoke of a family life once full and vibrant. Slow-roasted brisket, that Gran still swore came out best when she used the old cast-iron Dutch oven that had belonged to her own grandmother, warmed on the stove-top. She'd rubbed it the night before with coarse salt, cracked pepper, a palm full of granulated garlic, and just enough brown sugar to make the edges candy when the heat finally kissed it.

Next to the cutting board sat a mountain of creamy mashed potatoes— real ones, boiled with their jackets on, then riced while still steaming, folded with heavy cream, good butter, and a dangerous amount of roasted garlic that Gran carefully mashed with the back of a fork. A pat of butter melted into the crater on top, pooling gold.

There was a skillet of cornbread too, the top cracked and sugar-sanded the way Karl loved it. Gran had baked it in the same black skillet she used for everything else, so the bottom was leopard-spotted and crisp, the inside still faintly sweet from the memory of summer corn she'd frozen at its peak.

A bowl of her famous tomato-and-cucumber salad sat in the middle of the table, the tomatoes still sun-warm from the garden that morning, slicked with oil, cider vinegar, a pinch of sugar, and so much fresh dill it turned the whole thing emerald-flecked.

A large pitcher of fresh water stood next to it, and the coffee pot spewed fragrant steam as freshly ground beans brewed.

Gran didn't say much when they walked in—just wiped her hands on the apron that had once been red but was now faded pink from a thousand washings, and tilted her head toward the table already set with the good plates, the ones with the tiny blue flowers around the rim.

"Figured you two'd be half-starved after that train ride," she said, voice gruff the way love sounds when it's trying not to be obvious. "Eat before it gets cold. There's peach cobbler for after."

Keri sat as close to Karl as she could, their thighs brushing under the table, drawing strength from his presence as she struggled to stabilize her rattled emotions. The disappointment from Alex's cold reception lingered like a bitter taste, but she pushed it down, focusing instead on the man across from them. Alex lowered himself into a chair with a groan, his cane

40

propped against the table, and stared at his hands—gnarled and spotted with age, though he was not yet old.

Silence reigned as the meal progressed and Keri and Karl began to gain their bearings. Alex toyed with his food, but consumed very little of it between coughing spells. Finally, finishing what was on her plate, Gran addressed Keri.

"Tell me what's happened at the homestead while I've been gone. Has that stubborn lilac by the porch finally bloomed?" For a blessed half-hour the two women talked of ordinary miracles—new chicks, Red's latest tall tale, the way the morning glories had climbed clear to the roof. With every shared laugh, the tension in the room lost a little of its fire.

Conversation stayed determinedly light—Keri's careful questions about the early days and Gran's stories of colts born during a spring blizzard. Alex answered some of the questions in monosyllables, but he answered. When Gran passed the biscuits his way, their fingers brushed, and something almost tender flickered across his face, gone before it could settle.

At last, the plates were empty, or as empty as they would get. Gran and Keri rose together to clear the table and prepare to wash dishes. Karl waited until the clink of dishes filled the room, then slid his chair closer to his father.

"Pa," he said quietly, "we need to talk about the ranch."

The words fell into the room like a stone into still water. Alex's face crumpled—not with anger, but with a grief so deep it looked like surrender. His gnarled hands trembled on the oilcloth; the cane leaning against his knee rattled.

"I suppose the only thing to be done is sell," he whispered, voice thin as early fall ice. "Chester's the only hand left. Just a handful of cows."

Karl leaned in until their foreheads nearly touched. "Tomorrow we'll go over the ledgers, figure an asking price."

Alex's expression was still one of deep sadness. "Might not be enough to pay the debts, son. Might not be near enough."

"Don't let that trouble you." Karl's voice carried the steady ring of a man who had already fought this battle on a windswept train platform and won. "On the way here, the Lord showed me plain: the ranch never belonged to us in the first place, Pa. It's his spread, his cattle, his debts. We're just the hired hands. And hired hands don't carry the worry—only the work."

Alex searched his son's face with a look sharp enough to cut. Whatever

41

he saw there made him go very still. After a long moment, he murmured, "I think I need to lie down."

Karl helped him up, one strong arm around the wasting frame that had once lifted him onto his first pony. They moved slowly toward the little bedroom off the kitchen, Alex's slippers whispering over the floorboards like secrets.

In the quiet that followed, Keri's hands stilled in the soapy water. She told Gran everything—Red's tear-choked vow in the pre-dawn yard, Karl's revelation on the train, the certainty that grace was big enough to cover even consumption. When she finished, Gran's eyes brimmed over. She pulled Keri close, apron and all, and held her as if she were the child and Keri the comforter.

"It's so hard to understand what God is doing sometimes," Gran said against Keri's hair. "I've begged Him to heal Alex, to spare him this slow drowning. But I'm thankful—oh, child, so thankful—he's made the way clear to Karl. And to you."

Karl stepped back into the kitchen then, weariness and peace strangely mingled on his face. Gran turned to him, drying her hands on her apron.

"The church folk," she said. "Have you thought what they'll say when their preacher brings death itself into his house?"

Karl's smile was slight but sure. "I've thought of little else for a thousand miles. Some will call us fools. Some will keep their distance. A few might even ask me to step down." He shrugged, a gesture more eloquent than protest. "But the Lord didn't call me to be safe—he called me to be faithful. If he wants me preaching from a consumptive house, then that's where the pulpit will be. He'll handle the rest."

He crossed the room and rested his hands on Gran's shoulders. "We're not alone in this, Gran. Not one step."

Gran reached up and covered his hands with her smaller ones. "We need each other now more than ever."

Later, after the dishes were dried and the lamps turned low, Gran murmured, "You two must be worn out after your trip. Come on upstairs. I've got your room ready."

Relief flooded over Keri like a cool stream, and she eagerly rose to follow Gran toward the narrow stairs leading to the upper floor. Karl was a few steps behind, his hand brushing hers in a brief, reassuring touch. The stairs creaked under their weight, each step echoing the age of the house.

42

Gran paused at the top, her hand on the doorknob of the first room. "I made a special effort to clean and prepare your old room, Karl," she said, pushing the door open with a gentle creak. The room was modest but welcoming—a double bed with a hand-stitched patchwork quilt, a dresser topped with a washbasin and pitcher, and a small window overlooking the corrals. Dust motes danced in the last rays of sunlight filtering through the glass, and the air smelled faintly of lavender from sachets Gran must have placed in the drawers. On the wall above the washbasin hung a short length of horsehair rope. Sitting beside the basin was a crude carving of a horse.

Karl's eyes widened as he stepped inside, gazing around with a mix of nostalgia and surprise. "You left it all just as it was," he said, his voice thick with emotion. The walls held faded tintype photos of a younger Karl on horseback, and a shelf displayed boyhood treasures—a slingshot, a collection of arrowheads. He slipped to Gran's side and enveloped her in a hug, his broad shoulders dwarfing her slight frame. "Thank you for keeping my room up. I loved life on the ranch. There was a time when I thought I'd never leave here."

Gran patted his back, her eyes misty. "There's a wealth of memories in here. That quilt is made from some of the old shirts you and your pa wore. I had quite a time with each of 'em to find enough fabric for even small squares. And I knew you'd want to keep the horse." She paused, eyes growing misty. "Your pa could see from the start that horses were your true love. I don't think he ever carved anything else, but he was determined to give you that horse."

"And I'm glad you kept the rope," Karl said, as he smiled and lifted it off the nail. "I tried so many times to braid a rope; didn't think I'd ever get it done."

"You were only ten," Gran chuckled. "But I have to admit, I didn't think you'd get it done either!"

Gran turned to Keri, slipping an arm around her waist. "I'm sorry about the response from Alex. I didn't expect him to be quite so detached." She shook her head sadly.

"It makes me think I must have been something like that when you came to Yankton," Keri said. "Such deep sadness and no hope for the future,"

"You were in so much pain, then, Keri, but Alex seems to be caught up in something almost beyond despair. I've prayed and prayed, tried everything I know to do to help him, to discover what has such a strong hold on him.

43

But his sorrow is like a prison wall that keeps him in and everyone else out."

Keri's brow furrowed with concern. "Is it mostly because of losing the ranch?" She paused, gathering her thoughts before voicing the question that gnawed at her. "Is it because of me? Does he resent Karl bringing a stranger into the family at a time like this?"

Gran smiled warmly, though weariness lined her features. "It's sweet of you to ask, dear, but no. It's not you. Losing the ranch is a big blow—Karl's grandfather and great-grandfather poured their lives into building it from nothing but dreams and sweat. Alex feels angry, ashamed, and who knows what else when he thinks of the ranch. But he shouldn't. No one could have foreseen the devastation from last winter's blizzards. Cattle frozen in drifts, fences buried under snow—it was biblical in its fury. Combined with his failing health, it's too much for almost anyone to bear."

Karl leaned against the door frame, his arms crossed, eyes revealing a deep desire to bridge the gap with his father. "Does he really blame God for all this, or is he angry with me, too? For leaving? For not being here when things fell apart?"

Gran sighed, sinking onto the edge of the bed. "I don't think he's angry at any one thing or person," she replied thoughtfully. "He's probably most angry with himself. He has blamed God numerous times—shouted at the heavens, even. But I sense there's something deeper inside him that he's struggling with. I just have no idea what it is. He was always somewhat broody, even as a boy, keeping his thoughts locked away like treasures in a chest. But now, with the consumption eating at him day by day, it's like a new level of darkness has taken root."

Keri nodded, her mind racing back to her own journey of faith. She had been there, in that pit of despair, questioning why God allowed suffering. It was Karl and Gran who helped pull her out, with their quiet strength and unwavering belief. Now, perhaps it was her turn to help extend that same grace to Alex. "Maybe we can help him see that God hasn't abandoned him," she suggested softly. "That grace is still there, even in the shadows."

Gran reached out and squeezed Keri's hand. "That's the spirit, child. We'll need all the faith we can muster." She rose then, brushing down her apron. "I'll leave you two to settle in."

As Gran departed, closing the door behind her, Keri turned to Karl. He pulled her into his arms, holding her close, his chin resting on her head. "I'm sorry about Pa," he murmured. "I knew it might be rough, but his illness has progressed further than I expected."

Keri tilted her head up, meeting his gaze. "He's hurting, Karl. It wasn't that long ago that I was hurting a lot like that. It was yours and Gran's patience and kindness that We just have to show him love, even if he pushes it away."

He nodded, but his eyes held a storm of emotions—love, frustration, fear. "The ranch . . . it's worse than I thought. I can't say I really want to know how bad the bills are, but tomorrow we'll have to look it all over. Not looking forward to the next couple days."

"We have to keep our eyes on God through all of it," she said. "As you said, the ranch belonged to God all along. Perhaps our loss will be someone else's blessing."

They unpacked their few belongings in companionable silence, the room filling with the soft sounds of drawers opening and closing. Keri hung her dresses in the wardrobe, the fabric whispering like secrets, while Karl placed his Bible on the nightstand—a leather volume that had been his companion through recent trials and was beginning to show the wear. As they finished unpacking and the sun set fully, plunging the room into twilight, they knelt together by the bed, hands clasped in prayer.

"Lord," Karl began, his voice steady, "we thank you that we can know you are with us. Your presence is what we need above anything else. We are so grateful for the answers you provided for the many decisions that lie before us. We ask for comfort for Pa, physical and spiritual. Soften his heart. If healing isn't your plan for him, we ask for the blessing of peace in his soul. Mostly, please help us to be instruments of your grace in all these things. We willingly wait on you for direction. We humbly ask for wisdom and patience. You brought us to this point, this moment. We trust you've already given us everything we need to work through all that lies before us. We leave it all with you. Amen."

"Amen," Keri echoed, feeling a peace settle over her despite all that tomorrow might bring.

CHAPTER FOUR

Threads of the Quilt

The Wyoming sun painted the early September morning as it slipped up across the horizon, its radiance gilding the sagebrush and distant mountain peaks with a honeyed glow that seemed a gentle touch before the chill of autumn started setting in. Keri woke to the sound of roosters crowing, their sharp calls slicing through the chinked walls of the ranch house. The distant lowing of cattle served as a backdrop, a mournful chorus that carried the weight of a thousand sunrise on this land.

Karl was already up, dressing in his work clothes—faded jeans patched at the knees from years of kneeling in dirt, a flannel shirt soft from countless washings in lye soap, and sturdy boots caked with the red earth of the corral. "Gonna' check the fences with whatever hands are left," he said, his voice low and rough with lingering sleep. Kissing her forehead, he murmured, "You rest a bit more." His hand lingered on her cheek, callused thumb brushing her skin in a gesture so tender it made her chest ache. She was thankful they were able to weather this storm together.

But Keri couldn't linger. She watched out the bedroom window as Karl made his way to the barn, his broad shoulders cutting a familiar silhouette against the vastness. The flat landscape rolled away in every direction: tawny grasslands dotted with patches of grass drifting into final growth stages of deepening brown and muted reds, the colors of a land bracing for winter's bite. The silver thread of the corral fence, gnarled and twisted over the years by wind and sun, glinted in the warming light, each post a silent sentinel bearing scars from yesterday. Somewhere in the distance, a hawk cried—a lonely, piercing sound that echoed the hollow in her heart for this place she would never truly know.

She slipped on a simple calico dress, its faded blue flowers a hand-me-down from Gran, and a well-worn apron Gran had handed her last night, the fabric still holding the faint scent of yeast and hearth smoke. She swept her

46

hair up into a loose braid, strands escaping to frame her face like whispers of worry, and headed downstairs. The stairs creaked under her weight, a familiar groan that spoke of generations treading the same path.

Gran was slipping well-kneaded bread dough into a coated and flour-dusted pan, her practiced hands moving with the patient rhythm of a lifetime spent feeding souls as much as bodies. As she slipped her hands into warm dishpan water, suds clinging to her knuckles, she turned to greet Keri. "Mornin', dear. Coffee's on." The pot on the cast-iron stove bubbled with a low, insistent gurgle, releasing a plume of steam that carried the robust aroma of coarsely ground beans.

Keri filled a tin cup, the metal warm against her palms, and began to sip, savoring the familiar warmth that warmed her throat like liquid resolve. "How's Mr. Richmond this morning?"

Gran glanced toward the hallway leading to Alex's room, her eyes clouding with a mother's weary love. "Still abed. The nights are hard on him—coughing keeps him up, and frettin' wears him out even more." Her voice cracked just a fraction, betraying the fear she buried beneath layers of faith.

Keri nodded, her empathy stirring anew, a soft pang in her chest for the man crumbling behind that door. "Maybe I could bring him some breakfast? Try to talk?"

Gran's eyes softened, crinkling at the corners with unshed tears. "That might be just what he needs. But go gentle—he's often like a wounded animal, lashing out from pain." She reached out, squeezing Keri's hand with fingers gnarled from decades of wrangling dough and doubt alike.

Preparing a tray with oatmeal thickened with fresh cream from the morning's milking, toast slathered in chokecherry jam from last summer's harvest, and tea steeped weak to soothe his throat, Keri knocked softly on Alex's door. A gruff "Come in" granted entry, the words rasping like sandpaper. The room was dim, curtains drawn against the light to spare his aching eyes, the air thick with the scent of camphor rubbed on his chest and pine boards warmed by the morning sun. Alex sat propped up in bed on pillows, a small black book open on his lap—its leather cover cracked like the parched earth outside. As she entered, he quickly slapped the book covers shut and slipped it behind his pillow, his movements furtive, as if guarding a fragile secret.

"Morning, Mr. Richmond," Keri said softly, setting the tray on a side table scarred from years of bedside vigils. Steam curled up and over the oatmeal drizzled with cane molasses. The contents of the tin cup smoldered too. Alex peered at it, then questioned Keri, his voice a gravelly whisper.

"Coffee or tea?"

"Why, tea, I believe."

"Hmpffh!" Alex crossed his arms across his chest, the gesture pulling at the loose skin of his illness-wasted frame. "Can't convince Ma that my coffee ain't strong enough to do me harm." He shook his head.

Keri smiled, her heart twisting at seeing the spark of the man he once was. "I've heard about your coffee, Mr. Richmond. I believe Gran said it was boiled so strong it likely woke the neighbors up before you poured it." Alex quickly suppressed the tentative smile tugging at the corners of his mouth.

He eyed Keri warily, but something softened in his gaze. "Call me Alex. And, don't take this wrong, but I don't need any nursin'." His words were barbed, yet underneath lurked a plea—for dignity, for the strength he'd lost.

"This isn't really nursing, just making sure you have your breakfast before it gets cold." She pulled up a chair, the legs scraping against the floor like a sigh, sitting at a respectful distance. "Karl's out working already. He's determined to do everything he can to help with the ranch." She watched his face, seeing the flicker of pride warring with shame.

Alex picked mindlessly at his oatmeal, the spoon clinking against the bowl like out-of-control spurs. "Karl's got a higher callin' than this ranch." A melancholy expression captured his face, etching deeper lines around eyes that had once searched out the daily path for a dozen ranch hands.

"But he has a father that he loves, too." Her gentle comment made Alex raise his eyebrows and give her a piercing glance, raw with unspoken guilt.

"I don't reckon I deserve any affection from Karl. Maybe not from anyone." Alex let the statement hang, heavy as the tense silence that followed it. Keri scrambled for an appropriate response, her own sense of past guilt and regrets rising like ghosts.

"We can't earn someone's love." Her heart ached with the pangs of pain she recognized in Alex's eyes, like an impenetrable shadow that consumed any light that came near—a mirror to her own grief after Pa's death.

48

"Miss, you're mighty young to have so many answers." This time, his gaze nearly demanded a response from her, challenging yet desperate.

"The scripture says we can come to God and find grace in our time of need." Alex's eyes grew wide, a flicker of longing breaking through the despair. He dropped his head before speaking, voice barely audible.

"It does say that, doesn't it. Amazing grace," he whispered, a look of alarm rising in his eyes—as if grace were a wild thing he had reason to fear.

"Alex, after my pa died, it seemed like I'd lost everything in the world that mattered to me. I thought that God must have been angry with me, turned his back on me." She paused to gauge his response, her voice trembling with the memory of floodwaters and sudden emptiness.

"Your pa died?"

"Yes, I thought Gran might have told you."

Alex stared blindly for a moment, the room's shadows deepening his sorrow. "She might have."

"Pa had a heart attack; it took him while we were cleaning up after the flood. We thought God had spared us much heartache since the flood didn't take our new barn. But then . . . It makes you question everything." The words spilled out, laced with the saltiness of old tears.

Alex's gaze was fixed on Keri, a spark of connection igniting. "Question God, you mean?" Keri nodded, throat tight.

"It was Gran and Karl who helped me see that God wasn't mad at me. That's not why terrible things happen." Keri paused again. Alex watched her intently now, his breathing shallow. "And it's not why terrible things have happened to you. I don't understand everything that's happening in your life. I do know one thing. We can trust God and his grace."

Alex's eyes met hers for the first time, vulnerable as a colt's. He was silent for a long moment, then sighed, the sound ragged with years of buried grief. "Not sure God thinks I deserve any grace."

"None of us deserves it," Keri suggested gently, her voice a soothing balm. "He just gives it to us." She rose from the chair, heart full.

"Alex, I was mad at God the day I met Gran and Karl. And for a while, I wanted to hold onto that anger. But I realized if I didn't let go of it, God couldn't give me anything to replace it. I hope you'll let God give you what he has for you."

Alex didn't respond, but as she left, she noticed he was reaching for

49

the little black book again, his hands trembling slightly as he attempted to subtly open its covers—fingers seeming to caress the words on the pages.

The day unfolded with chores—Keri helping Gran in the garden, pulling weeds from the few vegetables still growing: stubborn carrots and late cabbages pushing through the soil. The earth was cool and crumbly under her nails, smelling of loam and faint onion from last year's crop. Tending to the chickens meant scattering grain amid a flurry of feathers and indignant clucks, their coop a ramshackle affair patched with tin from old cans. The physical labor was a welcome distraction, grounding her in the rhythm of ranch life—the creak of the windmill pumping water with a rhythmic groan, the distant echoing whinny of horses.

Karl returned at noon, dusty and sweaty, his shirt clinging to his back, reporting on the state of the fences. "Needs plenty of mending—but it would help with the sale, I think." His eyes met Keri's, a silent shared burden.

Lunch was simple—cornbread crumbly and golden from the Dutch oven, beans simmered with salt pork and a hint of molasses, coupled with Gran's good coffee to help ward off the advancing September chill that nipped at the edges of the open door. They had barely finished the last bite before a knock rattled the door, firm but not insistent.

Karl crossed the room in three strides and pulled it open. There stood Chester Harlan, hat clutched in his callused hands, knuckles scarred from branding irons and barbed wire. His weathered face creased with lines that spoke of sun and sorrow in equal measure, etched deeper by the dust of two decades riding this range. At forty-five, he was a fixture on the ranch, his dark hair silvering at the temples like frost on sage, his eyes the color of fertile earth after rain—warm, intelligent, holding secrets of the soil and sky alike. He'd come to the ranch as a young drifter nearly twenty years back, drawn by the promise of open spaces after losing his own kin to fever back East, and stayed because, as he often said with a quiet grin that crinkled his eyes, "This ground gets into a man's bones, same as the wind gets in your blood."

"Afternoon, Karl. Mrs. Richmond." His voice a low rumble, like thunder rolling over distant hills, Chester stepped inside the door, acknowledging both Gran and Keri with a nod that carried the weight of

50

shared hardships. He hung his hat on the peg by the door, the felt worn smooth from years of tipping to ladies and protecting from the sun and wind. "Didn't mean to trouble you folks, but . . . well, talk around here is that you're fixin' to sell the ranch, and I need . . ." He stumbled on his words, throat working as if swallowing dust, but quickly regained his composure, standing tall in boots polished only by prairie grit. "If what they're sayin' is true, I want to offer to buy it." His voice cracked on the last word, betraying the love he'd poured into this land like water into furrows.

Gran rose slowly, smoothing her apron with hands that trembled ever so slightly, her blue eyes sharp as ever despite the grief that shadowed them like clouds over the mountains. "Come sit, Chester. Kettle's still hot—can I get you some coffee?"

"Yes, coffee, if it's no imposition, ma'am, and . . ." Chester hesitated again, a flush creeping under his tan. "I hope you're the one who made it." Gran's chuckle burst out loudly, a rare bubble of joy amid the sorrow, as she turned to face Chester.

"Yes, you can rest easy," she answered, eyes twinkling with memory. "Alex hasn't been makin' any of his cowboy coffee lately—the kind that'd strip paint off a wagon."

Chester eased into a chair opposite Keri, the wood groaning under his solid frame, and nodded to Karl, who pulled up a stool beside the stove, its iron legs scraping like a fiddle's bow. The fragrance of freshly brewed coffee and lingering aroma of cornbread added a sense of comfort to the room, mingling with the faint scent of lye soap and sun-dried linens. It was the smell of home, fragile now.

Chester took the tin mug Gran pressed into his hands, wrapping his fingers around it as if to draw strength from the steam rising like morning mist off the creek. He met Karl's gaze first, then Gran's, his expression softening with a tenderness that made the room feel smaller, more sacred—a circle of souls bound by struggles and loss.

"Should Alex be part of this?" Chester's voice held the slightest quiver as he respectfully posed his question, his eyes flicking toward the hallway with the loyalty of an old trail dog. Gran and Karl exchanged glances, heavy with unspoken ache, and she answered.

"God bless ya' for askin', Chester, but the truth is, Alex is too sick to deal with anything regarding the ranch. He knows he's not able to continue, I'm too old, and Karl is following God's call. The talk you've heard is true. Karl and Keri came here to help settle things with the ranch and take me and Alex back to Dakota Territory." Her words hung like dust motes in the sunbeam slanting through the window.

Chester's expression registered surprise, his broad shoulders slumping a fraction. He leaned forward in his chair, elbows on knees. "Then I reckon' maybe I can be of help to ya'. The thing is—and I don't want to be disrespectful—after all the flooding, it's gonna' take time to rebuild this ranch. Or any ranch in these parts." Chester's gaze bounced from Gran to Karl to Keri. His words were deliberate, spoken with gentle precision. "And I don't know what ya'll have in mind regarding the debts against it. With all due respect, the mortgage may be more than the ranch is worth. I'm thinkin'—hopin'—we can work it all out." Chester's words trailed off with his last sentence, a mournful expression overtaking his weathered face, eyes glistening with the threat of tears he'd never shed in company.

Karl spoke up right away, voice steady but laced with emotion. "Chester, we thank you for all you've already done for this ranch, for Pa, for all of us. You've been like family all these years. I can't remember a time when you weren't here—fixin' breaks in the line shack or pullin' me out of the creek when I was fool enough to try swimmin' with the remuda."

Chester chuckled, a low, warm rumble like summer thunder, but it faded quickly. "I remember when you were born—tiny thing, squallin' like a coyote pup." Chester's smile turned to a frown, and the room was silent for a moment, the tick of the mantel clock marking heartbeats. "I know it broke your Pa's heart when your ma died. We were all so sorry to see how he took it—went out to the north pasture and didn't come back till dawn, sittin' with her grave marker like it answer his questions."

Karl and Gran exchanged glances as Gran spoke up, her voice thick. "I think the hardest part for Alex was not knowin' why she passed. She was so sickly for so many months—wasting away like autumn leaves. And then doctors couldn't decide what to do, just shook their heads and charged for the privilege."

"He was never the same after that," Karl added, his brow furrowing as memories flooded. "There was a sorrow about him that seemed beyond comfort. Almost like now." Karl wrinkled his brow as he spoke and sought Gran's gaze.

Chester nodded. "Somehow, it broke him. We could all see it— the way he'd stare at the horizon like it owed him answers." No one spoke for a moment, the weight of shared history pressing down. "I want you to know," Chester continued, voice dropping to a reverent hush, "we all would have liked to see your Pa recover from all this. But, if you don't mind me sayin' so, it appears that's not what God has in mind. I'm kinda' hopin' that it eases your Pa's mind some to know it's passin' to my hands—like passin' a torch that ain't gone out yet." Chester searched Karl and Gran for some sign of agreement, his own eyes misty with memories of better times.

"I think he will, Chester." Karl lowered his voice, emotion cracking through. "It eases the pain of letting go of our family's history on this place—if God hadn't called me out, I'd be the fourth generation here. We're not sure how long Pa has now, and we all need to get back to our own homestead at Yankton. It means a lot to us that you'd want to take over the ranch, and it certainly saves us a lot of time, not having to search for a buyer. I know you know every acre like your own heartbeat."

Chester flashed a quick smile. "And I don't mean to push, but winter's comin'. Snow'll be flyin' soon—" Chester's worry lines deepened.

"It's okay," Karl said, reaching across to clasp Chester's forearm. "We won't be taking any longer than we must in settling everything. If you can come back tomorrow at noon, we'll have some dinner—Gran's venison stew, maybe—and strike a deal. It's clear God's callin' us back to Dakota. We want to be fair with you."

Chester's wide grin revealed his relief, teeth flashing white against his tan, a rare unguarded joy. He reached for Karl's hand as he stood up to leave, pumping it a dozen times with the grip of a man sealing a covenant. "Surely appreciate it. This ranch… it's been my north star."

No one spoke as Chester walked out the door, his footsteps crunching on the gravel path worn smooth by boots and dreams. Gran finally stood and poured coffee for each of them before she spoke, the pot clinking against cups like a toast to endurance. "Are you ready to go over the bank records?" She peered over her tin cup at Karl, steam veiling her face.

"Not really ready, but willin'," he said, a wry smile tugging despite the dread. "I want Keri to sit in with us. If there's debt involved, she needs to know all the details—she's family now, in every way that counts." Gran nodded, pride and sorrow mingling in her eyes.

53

"Let's finish our coffee, and I'll get things set out on the desk—the one Elias built from cottonwood planks the year the railroad came through."

The Wyoming sun was dipping low, painting the sky in streaks of orange and pink as it settled down on the western horizon, the colors bleeding into the sage like wounds slowly healing. The old ranch house, weathered but proud, its log walls chinked with mud and memory, creaked softly in the breeze that accompanied the approaching evening—a wind that carried the scent of cooling earth and distant pine. Inside, the parlor glowed with the flicker of a single oil lamp, its flame dancing like the spirits of roundups past. Keri sat on the edge of a worn settee, horsehair stuffing peeking through threadbare upholstery, her hands folded in her lap, watching Karl and Gran as they stood by the stone hearth blackened from decades of pine and cow chip fires. The air smelled of pine resin and the faint tang of leather from the saddles stacked in the corner, oiled and ready for rides that would never come again.

Karl leaned against the mantel, his broad shoulders filling out the flannel shirt he'd worn since dawn, now streaked with the day's labor. His dark hair was tousled, and his eyes—hazel like his father's—carried a weight heavier than his years, shadowed by the legacy pressing in. Gran, her silver hair pulled into a tight bun secured with bone pins carved by her own father, sat in her rocking chair, a quilt draped over her knees despite the warmth of the fire—patchwork squares salvaged from dresses of wives and daughters long gone.

The pall that had threatened since Keri and Karl arrived at the ranch now blanketed them in a cloud of resigned sorrow, thick as the smoke from a branding fire. What they had dreaded may be true was a sad reality. The ranch, three generations deep in their blood—staked in '49 with nothing but a wagon, a rifle, and faith—was slipping away. Tomorrow, the banker would come with papers to collect payment on the mortgage and sign it over to Chester, the ink drying like blood on a contract. Alex lay frail in the back room, his cough a constant reminder echoing through the thin walls, evidence of the choice they must make.

Gran's voice broke the silence, soft but steady, laced with the tremor of held-back tears. "This house has seen more than its share of joy, Karl. Remember the winter of '61? When the snow piled so high we couldn't open the front door, and the wolves howled so close we kept the rifle by the bed?"

54

Karl's lips twitched into a half-smile, eyes distant with boyhood wonder. "I was barely walking then, Gran. You tell that story better than I could live it." But his voice caught, remembering the warmth of her lap during those storms.

She chuckled, the sound like dry leaves rustling in a gentle breeze, warm with affection. "Your pa and your granddad shoveled a path to the barn for three days straight, beards iced over like Santa Claus. Found old Bessie the milk cow half-buried in a drift, still chewing her cud like nothin' was wrong, her breath steamin' in the cold."

Keri leaned forward, drawn in despite herself, the stories wrapping around her like a shawl. "Bessie sounds like she had spirit."

"Oh, she did," Gran said, eyes sparkling with tears that caught the lamplight. "Kicked more than one cowboy into the dirt—sent young Chester flyin' once, landed him in the water trough with a splash that echoed to the hills. But she gave the sweetest cream you ever tasted, thick enough to stand a spoon in. Churned butter that won ribbons at the county fair in Laramie."

Karl pushed off the mantel, crossing to the window where the last light glinted off the corral, painting the twisted rails in fire. "The roundups and trail rides . . . they're what I'll miss most." His voice was low, almost reverent, cracking with the love of a boy who'd grown into a man on their backs. "This ranch raised me as much as you and Pa did, Gran. Every sunrise ride, every thunderstorm scatter—they're in my blood."

"Tell Keri about Thunder," Gran prompted, rocking gently, the chair's creak a lullaby of yesteryears.

Karl's smile grew, though it didn't reach his eyes, shadowed by impending loss. "Thunder was Granddad's pride. Black as midnight, with a white blaze like a lightning strike down his face. Ornery as sin, too. Threw me into the water trough when I was twelve, trying to break him. I came up spitting mud and fury, and Granddad just laughed, said, 'Boy, you gotta' earn his respect, same as any wild thing.'" Karl's fingers traced the windowpane, as if touching the memory.

"Did you?" Keri asked, her voice soft, heart aching for the boy he'd been.

"Eventually." Karl turned from the window, his gaze distant, voice thick with pride and sorrow. "Took two years. I'd sneak out to the corral at dawn, just sit on the fence and talk to him—about Ma, about the stars,

55

about nothin'. Apples helped, sliced thin so he'd take 'em from my palm without bitin'. By the time I was fourteen, he'd let me ride. Fastest horse we ever had—could outrun a prairie fire, hooves thundering like judgment day. We drove cattle clear to Cheyenne one spring, three hundred head kickin' up dust that choked the sun. Thunder was the horse you wanted if you were keeping the herd tight, cuttin' off strays with a glance."

Gran nodded, a tear slipping free. "Your granddad said Thunder chose you, not the other way around. Same way this land chose us, back when my pa staked the claim in '49—nothin' but sage and sky, and a promise to make it bloom."

Karl's jaw tightened, emotion rippling like heat over the plains. He moved to the fireplace, picking up a small, worn horseshoe from the mantel—rusted, bent from Thunder's hoof. "Then there was Daisy," he said, voice quieter now, reverent as prayer. "Pa's mare. Gentle as a lamb, but strong—dapple gray with a mane like silk. She carried me when I was too small to keep up on the range, my legs danglin' like twigs. Taught me how to read the wind, how to feel the herd's rhythm in my bones." He turned the horseshoe in his hands, the iron cool against his calluses, a talisman of simpler days. "She's out in the pasture now, too old to work, grazin' slow under the cottonwoods. I can't bear to think of her with strangers—her soft nicker when I'd bring sugar cubes, the way she'd rest her head on my shoulder like a child."

Gran reached out, her gnarled hand resting on his arm, veins like river maps. "We've had good years here, Karl. More than most. Your pa and all of us, we built somethin' with sweat and love—and tears enough to irrigate the badlands. You'll carry that, wherever you go, in the set of your shoulders, the way you gentle a horse."

Keri's throat tightened, a lump rising as if the ranch's spirit pressed against her ribs. Karl and Gran were her only connection to the ranch, yet their grief felt like her own, raw and shared. "The ranch . . . it's more than land, isn't it?" she said, almost to herself, voice trembling with the weight of inheritance.

Karl met her eyes, and for a moment, the weight in his lifted, love shining through like sunlight on water. "It's been home. Every hoofprint in the dust, every creak in these floors from boots comin' in at dusk. It's who we are, at least who we were." His hand found hers, squeezing with quiet promise. "We have to remember what God says to Isaiah in chapter

56

43. Let go of the former things, don't dwell on the things of yesterday. I'm doing a new thing."

Gran's rocker stilled. She let the silence settle like dust after a herd's passing, then spoke, voice low and steady, as if she was gentling a skittish colt.

"Karl, your granddad marked that passage with a burnt matchstick the year the creek ran dry. Said it was God's promise we'd never thirst for hope, even when we didn't see God provide what we expected. There's been times here when this land was a wilderness, but God led us through. When we walk away, we're taking the most valuable thing we ever had here: God's presence."

Outside, the wind picked up, rattling the shutters like restless ghosts, carrying the scent of cooling sage and distant rain. Karl's gaze went well beyond the ranch house walls. "I just wish Pa could've seen one more roundup," he said, voice barely above a whisper, breaking. "One more sunrise over the herd, the cattle lowin' like a hymn, coffee boilin' on the fire."

Gran's eyes glistened, but her voice held firm, an anchor in the storm. "There's a day comin' when we'll all be enjoyin' God's creation like we've never imagined. It will come."

The fire crackled, casting shadows across the room that danced like memories. Keri watched them, these two bound by blood and memory, and felt the ranch's heartbeat in the walls around them—a pulse as steady as the horses Karl would never forget, as enduring as the faith that had carried them through drought and death.

As the coffee cooled and the stars pricked the velvet sky beyond the window, the three of them lingered, voices weaving tales of yesterdays and hopes for the dawn—stories of branding days when the air rang with laughter and the sizzle of iron, of Christmas with a pine bough dragged in from the hills, adorned with popcorn strings and paper stars. In that simple kitchen, amid the scent of woodsmoke and resolve, the ranch found not an end, but a quiet resurrection in their hearts.

The western sky was painted in rose pinks and muted blues by the time Gran came back to the kitchen from checking on Alex, her steps slower, as if each one cost her a piece of soul. Her lips, usually set in a firm line of resolve, were softened into a faint, wistful curve—not quite a smile, but a tender acknowledgment of the life she had lived on the ranch for so many years, from bride to matriarch. Her cheeks, weathered by years of sun and wind that had tanned her like saddle leather, seemed to sag slightly, as if the strength that held them high had now ebbed under the tide of memories—floods, births, burials under the pines.

Her eyes, once sharp and commanding as a hawk's, shimmered with a delicate sheen, like dew on morning grass after a frost. As she stood by the kitchen sink, her gaze drifted across the familiar expanse. Keri, following closely behind Gran, slipped her arm around the matriarch's shoulders.

"It will be difficult when it's time to go." It took a moment for Gran to respond to Keri's statement.

"So many memories here," she said. "When Elias and I first took over the ranch, he had some doggone stubborn mules. I tell you all they ever did was kick up dust. But Elias swore they were the best thing to survive this rugged country. He was right about that. And you see that little ridge just beyond the garden fence? That's how big our first gardens were. I taught Alex how to plant seeds right there. His hands were too small at first to grip a hoe. When Karl came along, it was Alex who helped him learn to garden. I think I'll miss the porch most of all. That's where Elias and I watched many a sunset as we finished our evening coffee."

It wasn't in Gran to weep openly, but her eyes lingered, tracing the contours of a place she knew now she'd never see again in the same way, each blade of grass a farewell.

Keri's heart was heavy with empathy, well aware of Gran's melancholy state, sensing it in the slight quiver of her shoulders. The air about Gran was heavy, almost palpable, as if the ranch itself was exhaling its own farewell, the wind through the eaves sighing like a lament. Gran stood still and quiet at the window, her posture slightly stooped, not from age but from the gravity of letting go—the weight of leaving the grave of her husband, the birthing stall where foals first stood on wobbly legs.

Keri hesitated to interrupt whatever thoughts Gran was experiencing, visions perhaps of roundups and river crossings. As always, there was a quiet dignity in Gran's presence, a stoic grace that spoke of resilience tempered by tenderness, forged in the fire of frontier trials. Gran's hands, clasped loosely before her, fidgeted with the edge of her apron, a small, unconscious gesture that betrayed the ache in her heart—the same apron that had wiped tears and flour in equal measure. Still, there was a trace of peace in her quiet posture, as if she was already beginning to cradle the memories she would carry forward, even as she left the land behind, like seeds in her pocket for a new garden.

As she turned, Gran managed a faint smile for Keri, eyes crinkling with affection that pierced the gloom. "It's been a rough afternoon, wouldn't you say?" Gran moved to the shelf to grasp the coffee tin, the metal cool in her hands, a ritual to steady the tremor.

"I'm so sorry you're having to go through this." Keri was struggling with her own frayed emotions as she considered the all-too-familiar pain of losing something so dear to the heart—the barn that survived the flood, nearly lost to another. Gran moved to hug Keri, her embrace fierce despite her frailty, smelling of soap and sage.

"We have each other to help get through this," Gran whispered, voice muffled in Keri's hair. "But it's going to hurt like birthin' a breach calf. I'm thankful I have someone as sweet and strong as you and Karl going through it with me—you with your quiet faith, him with his stubborn hope."

The heavy thud of Karl's boots interrupted them as he walked into the kitchen. "Gran, I reckon it's time I sat down with Pa and laid it all out straight: what's become of the ranch, the sale, and this long ride back to the homestead. You know how the railroad is. They'll insist he rides in the cattle car with the stock. They'll never let him ride in the coach car. It will be me and him back there in the whole way, breathin' dust and straw, listenin' to the bawlin' of steers and the rattle of the wheels on the rails. We'll need every quilt we can carry, the heavy ones Mama pieced before she passed, to pile around him so the cold don't sink clear into his bones. And food, well, I'll pack what I can: a slab of that salt pork, some cold cornbread, a jar of your peach preserves if there's any left. Though truth be told, I doubt he'll take more'n a bite or two."

Gran placed her hand on her mouth to conceal the painful emotion the words brought on. Her whole body stiffened as she grasped Keri's hand and said, "Yes. We need to do all we can to help Alex get through this."

The lamp burned low in the small bedroom, its flame trembling against the drafts that slipped through the log walls. Karl sat on the edge of the narrow bed, elbows on his knees. Alex lay propped against the headboard, thin shoulders swallowed by a nightshirt that had once fit him snug. His breathing came in shallow pulls, each one a small fight.

Gran stood at the foot of the bed, arms folded over her apron, eyes

59

never leaving her son's face. Keri hovered in the doorway, a shawl around her shoulders, holding a tin cup of willow-bark tea that had long since gone cold.

Karl cleared his throat. "Pa… Mr. Harlan come by this afternoon. Chester Harlan."

Alex's eyes, still bright in his thin, disease-ravaged face, turned toward his son.

"He wants the place," Karl went on, voice low. "All of it. The north range, the creek pasture, even the old line shack. We talked a long time. He made a fair offer—more'n fair. I shook on it."

A cough rattled in Alex's chest. He pressed the quilt to his mouth until it eased.

Gran spoke first, quiet but steady. "It's the Lord's timing, Alex. Land don't mean nothin' if it costs you the only family you got left."

Alex managed a faint nod.

"Papers'll be ready day after tomorrow," Karl said. "Soon as the ink's dry and the bank's settled, we're leavin'. All four of us. Gran's already packing. Morning train east—back to Yankton, to the homestead. We are all family now, Pa. We take care of each other—no matter the miles or the storms." His words were a vow, tender yet fierce.

Alex stared hard at Karl before glancing away and gazing at unseen entities—ghosts of failures past. "Family." The word oozed pain, enough to make everyone else flinch, a raw wound exposed. Still staring off into space, Alex murmured, "You may not want to be part of my family." The confession hung, heavy with unspoken secrets.

"Pa, please." Karl stood and moved closer to his father's side, kneeling to look into his face, hand on a bony shoulder. "You have to tell us what's eating at you. What is it that's so painful it's draining every bit of life in you."

A haunting expression of grief and misery fell across Alex, and a few sparse tears filled his tired eyes, tracing paths through the stubble on his cheeks. "I know we have to sell the ranch. I've known I've failed. Failed you, Karl, Ma, Pa, and Grandpa" He hung his head, sorrow causing him to shrink into himself physically and spiritually, a giant reduced to ash. "The worst of it is . . ." He raised his eyes to meet Karl's, wild with desperation, but no more words came.

Keri trembled, her gaze riveted on Karl, who fixed his empathetic gaze

60

on Alex, love unwavering.

"Whatever it is, we'll work through it, Pa. God will show us the way. He always has." Alex was silent, immense grief still capturing his expression, but a flicker of relief softened the edges.

Keri stepped forward and set the cup on the dresser. "I'll see to it that we gather all your things, too. If there's anything special, you want to take along just let us know." Her voice wobbled as she finished the sentences.

Karl leaned closer. "Pa, you know how the railroad is. They won't let a man as sick as you ride in the coach car. Folks get scared of the consumption."

"I've seen it," Alex rasped. "Turned away at the ticket window."

Gran moved to the bedside and laid her work-worn hand over Alex's. "So you and Karl will ride in the cattle car. I'm sorry it has to be that way, but it's warmer than the platform, and it's only one night."

Keri knelt, gathering quilts from the chest. "I'm sewing a lining of flannel inside your coat, Alex, with a double layer across the chest."

Karl gave her a grateful look, then turned back to his father. "Straw on the floor, slats for walls, cold as sin once we cross the river—but Gran's giving us every quilt in the house. I'll bundle you so tight the wind won't know where to bite."

Gran straightened, practical as always. "I'll be boilin' a gallon of coffee with chicory and an egg in it—thick enough to keep its heat. I'll pour it scalding into two stone jugs, wrap 'em in gunny sacks and quilts, and we'll bury 'em deep in the straw. It'll still be drinkable for most of that first day."

Alex's eyes grew misty. He looked past Karl to his mother. "Thank you, Ma. Ain't had real coffee in weeks."

Gran's mouth trembled, but she only said, "You'll have it every day once we're home."

Keri brushed a lock of gray hair from Alex's forehead. "And I'm bringing the feather pillow you like. Railroad straw's full of stickers. You'll rest your head soft, Alex."

Karl squeezed Alex's hand. "We have a new home now, and we'll make it together, Pa. Same as always.

Alex reached out a trembling hand and laid it on his son's wrist. His fingers were hot with fever, but the grip was still there, stubborn as ever. "Together," he whispered.

61

Gran leaned down and pressed her lips to Alex's brow, the way she had when he was small. Keri slipped her arm gently around Karl's shoulders, resting her cheek against his sleeve.

Outside, the Wyoming night pressed against the windows, vast and starlit, but inside the little room, the lamp burned steady now, fed by Gran's quiet hand, holding the dark at bay for now.

CHAPTER FIVE

Shadows of Sorrow

The wagon creaked to a halt in the yard just as the early September sun dipped behind the cottonwoods, painting the homestead in bruised purples and golds.

"Alex, we're here." Gran slipped her arm around her son's shoulders. Alex was blanket-wrapped, thinner than the fence rails he'd once split with his own hands. A cough rattled in his chest—wet, stubborn. Karl quickly stepped to the back of the wagon and offered his arm. Alex waved it off, independent as ever, but his knees buckled as he stepped to the ground. Keri slipped under his elbow before he could protest, feeling the fever-heat through his coat. "Easy, Pa," Karl murmured. "You're home now."

Home. The word hung in the air like chimney smoke. Alex's eyes— hazel tones dulled with illness—lifted to the barn. Keri had watched men appraise land, cattle, even brides, but never a building the way Alex looked at that barn. Its gambrel roof rose proud against the prairie, the loft door yawning open like a promise.

Alex drew in a breath. "That's the barn yer' pa built?"

"He drew it first," Keri said. "He dreamed of it when he was just a boy. God blessed him and allowed him to build it."

A ghost of a smile cracked Alex's dry, chapped lips. "That was quite a dream." He dropped his head and didn't speak as they made their way to the house.

Keri slipped aside and scurried to the barn, where the main door was flung open. Inside, the four mares and two weanlings quietly munched their grain. Keri slipped up beside each one, embracing, petting, and sharing her joy at returning home.

"Gracie, you are looking so beautiful," Keri cooed to the mare. "I can see Red took good care of you this past month."

"Not just good care, great care, I'll have you know!" Red gave Keri a quick hug and a delighted smile. "How is Alex?"

"Come and meet him. He could use some of your cheer, I'm sure. The train trip was hard on him, especially after the sale of the ranch. My heart goes out to him. I know that sick feeling of losing everything you hold dear. He needs a lot of healing."

"We've all been praying here. I hope Karl don't mind that I've been keepin' folk at church informed about how things were goin'."

"Not at all, Red. We are grateful for all your help, and the Lord knows Alex and all of us need all the prayers we can get. Are you done with chores?"

"Pret' near," Red answered. "I'll be in shortly. Let me know if there's anything you need. We are all—" he gestured toward the horses—"happy to see you."

Keri hurried to the house to see what needed to be done to get a much-anticipated hot meal on the table. They had traveled lightly on the train, including in terms of food. She was certain everyone else, like herself, was ready for a sumptuous meal.

For one moment, she stopped and turned a complete circle to take in the sight of the homestead. The cottonwoods were taking on a golden hue as summer faded and transitioned to fall. Tall grasses rattled in the slight breeze, their drying and hollow stems creating a natural symphony for anyone nearby. The chickens had already retreated close to the coop as the afternoon sun's brilliance and warmth faded, and the milk cow stood patiently at the barn door, waiting for milking time. The brilliant blue of the prairie sky was quickly softening to a muted pastel as the sun's rays shortened and paled. The subtle daily changes they had missed for these weeks now brushed the landscape with a fresh autumn look.

As she bounded up the porch steps, Keri heard laughter ringing in the kitchen. Even though unexpected, she was comforted by the sound of the chuckles. As she slipped inside the door, she was greeted by the sight of Gran and Karl standing next to Alex, all three wearing wide smiles and sipping coffee. The inquisitive look on her face caught Gran's attention first.

"Is Red in the barn?" Gran asked, regaining her composure. Keri nodded. "Well, he's comin' in for supper, right?" Keri nodded again as Gran turned to Alex. "You'll have to compare your coffee recipe with Red

64

when he gets here. Strong enough to float a horseshoe. That's a good one, Alex."

Keri's heart warmed to see the glint of mirth in Alex's eyes, the corners of his mouth twitching upward in a rare, unguarded smile. Still, his eyes were misty. For the past thirty hours, as the train sped them on their way home, he had spoken scarcely a word, as if he needed every bit of energy he had to endure the ride. It seemed God had nearly overloaded this shell of a man with loss and sorrow—the sale of the ranch that had been his father's and grandfather's before him, the hasty bundling of a life into two worn satchels and a battered trunk, the long, tense ride on the train from Laramie to Yankton. Every mile had etched itself into the hollows beneath his eyes. The trauma of her own father's death and near loss of the homestead was still so fresh in her heart and mind. Alex surely must be pushing down sorrowful and anguished thoughts that were likely to be settling in his heart. It was easy to imagine that the uncertainty of whatever lay ahead in Dakota pressed on him.

Help me know how to bring comfort to him. Keri whispered the prayer to herself as she surveyed the kitchen, preparing to help with supper.

"Keri, Red's got a bit o' fire goin' here so let's get some soda-biscuits ready for the oven and I'll get some stew on. If everybody's as hungry as I am after that train ride, we'll be chasin' down some chickens before we're done!" More chuckles rippled through the room at Gran's words as the fragrance of stew and biscuits quickly swallowed up the aroma of Red's stout coffee.

The aroma of the meal began filling the kitchen when Red burst in the door. He slapped his hat on the hook beside all the rest and started making the rounds with hugs and hellos. "Alex," Red said, extending his hand in friendship. "I've heard a lot about you. I'm right sorry for all your troubles. I know we are all happy to have you here with us. You have a splendid family here who want to help give you everything you need."

Eyes wide and the hint of a smile on his lips again, Alex received Red's handshake, mumbling his thanks and appearing surprised at Red's warmth.

Gran turned from the stove to Red and Alex as she said, "Red, you've met your coffee-makin' match here. You and Alex are gonna' have us all drinkin' pure grounds I think before we're done. I know Alex will enjoy hearing your coffee-makin' story."

Red chuckled as he pulled a chair up next to Alex. Red's burly frame and radiant complexion were a stark and telling contrast to Alex's paper-thin skin and dwindling health.

"First time I ever made coffee," he drawled, "I was sixteen and green as spring grass. Pa had sent me up to the line shack with old Zeke—meanest cook west of the Pecos and twice as ugly. Zeke hands me a sack of Arbuckle's and a pot blacker than sin and says, 'Boy, coffee's the only thing keeps a man alive out here. Don't come back till you can make it strong enough to wake a hibernatin' grizzly in winter.'"

Red paused as laughter rippled around the room.

"So I figure, strong means strong. I dump in half the sack—grounds thick as creek mud—set it on the hottest part of the stove, and wait. Ten minutes in, that pot starts jumpin' like a frog on a griddle. Zeke's snorin' in the corner, so I poke the pot with a stick. Bad idea. Lid blows clean off, coffee shoots up like Old Faithful, paints the ceiling, drips down Zeke's beard. He comes up cussin' in three languages, face lookin' like a drowned badger."

Alex laughed out loud. Karl and Gran exchanged smiles.

"Zeke grabs the pot, takes a swig—straight, no cup—and his eyes go wide as supper plates. Says, 'Boy, you done murdered the bean, but be darned if it ain't alive!' Then he laughs so hard he can't talk. Hands me the pot and says, 'From now on, that's your coffee. Call it Red's Resurrection—wakes the dead and keeps the livin' humble.'" Red and Alex both laughed as Alex slapped Red on the back.

"Been brewin' it near the same ever since. Use almost half a sack, boil till it sings, let the grounds settle like rocks in a stream. Ain't fancy, but it'll put hair on your chest and truth in your soul. And if it don't float a horseshoe…then I ain't Red."

Everyone laughed as Red finished his tale, and Alex said, "I told you, Ma. It'd float a horseshoe!" A wave of mirth and relief swept over the kitchen. Keri noted that, for the first time since she met him, the shadow of pain in Alex's eyes was nowhere to be seen.

Gran and Keri slipped plates and silverware onto the table and soon began plopping fine-smelling dishes into the center of the table.

"Karl, I believe we're ready for grace." Hands on her hips, Gran surveyed the table and everyone sitting around it. Karl nodded, bowing his head as Gran took her place. The lamplight flickered across the rough-hewn table and the faces gathered round it—Gran's silvered hair, Alex's

66

gaunt frame propped in the corner chair, Keri's hands folded beside his own, and Red's mirthful presence next to Alex. The scent of venison stew and fresh soda-biscuits rose like a quiet offering. When the room stilled, Karl's voice came low and steady, the cadence of a man who'd prayed over branding fires and open graves alike.

"Heavenly Father, we set this table in the home you have provided and on a new path you've shown us tonight, but we set our hearts on the same Rock that carried us here. We thank you for showing us your plan for the ranch—hard as it was to let go, you made a way through Chester's willing hands. We thank you for the safe travel across miles of sagebrush to this river bottom. We thank you for the promise that you'll lead us through each coming day—through joy and trial, according to your will and purpose for each one of us. Lord, tune our ears to your voice, give us obedient hearts—quick to follow, slow to fret. May we walk the steps you mark out, whether they run straight or wind through wilderness. We ask all this in the name of Jesus, who makes every new path a homeward trail. Amen."

A single kerosene lamp burned steady on the rough plank table, its glow catching the steam that rose from the enamel pot of stew. The room was hushed; even the fire in the little sheet-iron stove seemed to listen.

Everyone took their first bites of the meal in a reverent silence. Alex was the first to speak. "I thank ya' for the prayer, son." His voice was tremulous, weak but immersed in emotion. "Seems like it's somethin' I maybe been needin' to hear." The words proceeded another stillness. "And it's kinda' helpin' me get over Red's coffee." Laughter filled the room again.

"Now, some people say I can cook but they don't mention bein' a good cook," Red chimed in. "Besides. You all know it's a sin to make weak coffee."

As Alex passed the biscuits to Karl, his gaze lingered on his son. "Karl." His voice, raspy and unsteady. "Thank you for bringin' me to your home. I'll do all I can to make myself welcome here."

Karl's gaze softened. "Pa, you are always welcome here. No matter what." Alex locked his gaze on Karl for what seemed forever, his eyes searching, almost pleading. As Alex replied, tears welled up in his eyes. "Thank you." He dropped his head and stared at the bits of food on his plate. Gran broke the awkward silence.

67

"Alex, we're putting you in Karl's old room. No steps. It's right beside mine. That way it'll be easy for you to get around some."

Red laid his hand on Gran's arm before he spoke. "If it sounds okay, Alex, I'll bring you out to the barn tomorrow so you can see these beautiful Belgian horses that God has seen fit to bless us with." Gran nodded in agreement, and Alex glanced at Keri.

"They told me about the Belgians," Alex said. "You're a mighty little gal to be handling them horses, if they're as big as Karl and Gran said."

Keri smiled. "They are big, but they're hearts are so gentle. Anyone who knows and cares about horses can handle them. They're always willing to do whatever we ask."

"Alex, I think it's time we get you some rest." Gran pushed away from the table and came to Alex's side. His pale face and trembling hands revealed the toll the long day had taken. Karl rose to help him find his way to his bedroom.

The last dish clinked into the dry dishpan, and the lamplight thinned to a soft gold. Karl and Gran had eased Alex down the short hallway, the bedroom door closing with a quiet click.

Keri lingered at the table, tracing the grain of the pine with one fingertip. Red sat opposite, hat in his lap, thumbs rubbing the sweat-stained brim the way another man might worry a rosary.

"He didn't eat enough to keep a sparrow alive," Red murmured, voice pitched low so the walls wouldn't carry it. "Consumption don't give a man second chances on an empty belly."

Keri's eyes lifted, steady but glistening. "The doctor in Laramie said the same. Lungs fill, strength seeps out—day by day, like sand through a sieve. Most folks don't climb back up that hill." She pressed her lips together, then added softer, "No one knows the number of his days, Red. Only the Lord."

Red nodded slow, gaze on the cooling coffee between them. "Body's one battle. Soul's another. I watched his eyes tonight—hollow-like. Whatever's eatin' him ain't just the sickness."

Keri folded her hands, knuckles whitening. "There's a weight he carries alone, Red. Guilt, maybe. Shame. He was in his bedroom reading a little black book the first morning we were there—leather cracked, pages worn soft. When I walked into the room, he snatched it away quickly, like he was afraid to be seen with it."

Red's brow lifted. "Bible?"

"Could be. Or a journal. I didn't ask Karl or Gran. I wanted to respect his privacy." She swallowed. "If that book holds what's strangling his heart, maybe mercy's waiting on the other side of speaking about it."

Red leaned forward, elbows on the table. "Fear'll tell a man to keep the lid nailed tight. Grace says pry it open and let the light in." He gently tapped the scarred wood. "You tell Karl about it. Not to pry, but to pray. And if the time comes Alex wants to hand that book over or speak about what's in it, you'll be ready to receive it —arms open. No questions till he's ready."

Footsteps sounded in the hall. Karl appeared first, shoulders sagging with the day's miles; Gran followed, apron twisted in her hands. The lamplight caught the worry etched around their eyes.

Keri rose, smoothing her skirt. "He's settled?"

"For now," Karl said, voice rough. "Sleepin' hard, or tryin' to."

Gran's gaze moved between Keri and Red, reading the air. "Somethin' on your hearts?"

Keri glanced at Red; he gave the smallest nod. She drew a breath. "Just prayin' the Lord loosens what's bound up in Alex—body and soul both."

Gran's eyes softened, and she reached for Keri's hand. "God's been talkin' to that boy ever since I can remember. If he's ever gonna' respond, it will have to be soon. Maybe it's finally time for the hinges on that door of his heart to give way."

Red pushed back his chair, the scrape soft against the split log floor. "I'll check the horses before I bed down. I'll be prayin' Alex has a restful night. Whatever God has for him in the coming days, he's not alone now."

The mid-September sunrise was warm and bright as high, thin clouds sat like blankets over the blazing golden star. Red held Alex's elbow as they made their way down the porch steps behind Keri.

"Take your time, Alex." Red gave a light, affirming squeeze to Alex's arm as Alex came to a halt.

"You know," Alex said between wheezes and coughs, "it's been a long time since I was excited to see something, and this barn interests me more than anything I can remember." Red smiled. "Did you help build the barn, Red?"

"I helped Keri's Pa, but he did most of the work. He was a skilled builder, and I think he considered every detail that would make a horse barn valuable, didn't he, Keri?"

Keri gave a delighted chuckle. "I think you're right, Red. All he ever wanted was to raise horses and build this barn."

"Why did he want Belgian horses?"

Keri's face wrinkled as she thought about Alex's question.

"He believed that new settlers here would find the breed hardy enough to break sod," she said. "They're strong and gentle. That was one thing Pa greatly admired in our mares. They have such willing hearts."

As they stepped into the cool shade of the barn, Alex let his eyes travel along the beams and stalls with the slow, practiced gaze of someone who had spent decades judging livestock shelters by how well they protected both animals and investments. He gazed up at the precisely placed beams that formed a wooden skeleton for the pine that shaped the building.

His words came between spells of coughing and wheezing. "Your pa had quite a vision. How long did it take to build this?"

"Nearly a year," Keri answered. "Pa worked long days every chance he had. It was the only thing that kept us from being swept away in the floodwater."

"Those stalls look twelve-by-twelve."

"Yes," Keri said. "Pa wanted to be sure we could stall a mare and her colt without having either horses or us squeezed in."

"So where are the horses?"

"Here's one." Red led Gracie up into her stall, where a mouthful of grain lay in the feedbox. Gracie immediately stuck her nose in the box and started munching. Keri locked arms with Alex and steadied him as they walked up beside the mare.

Wide-eyed, Alex reached out to stroke the mare's side and creamy mane. "I'll be darned. No wonder your Pa wanted to raise these horses. That is one beautiful mare. What's her name?"

"Gracie." Keri and Red watched as Alex moved closer to Gracie, gently patting her and murmuring admiringly. "She was Pa's favorite, and mine too."

Alex's eyes were shining as a hush fell over the barn. "My granddad broke sod with oxen," he whispered. "Took three days to turn an acre. These girls could do it by supper."

Gracie turned to nudge Alex, causing Red to step up between them quickly. "Easy girl," Red said. "You've had enough grain for the moment."

Alex smiled, coughed, and leaned back against the stall wall behind him.

"Pa—I mean, Alex! Are you okay?" Keri stepped close to help Alex

70

retain his balance and ensure he wasn't injured or alarmed. The expression in his eyes was soft, still, as if every former worry had finally loosened its grip and something quiet and glad had moved in to stay. For a moment, the consumption, the shame, the secret that gnawed his heart—all of it fell away. There was only the warmth of a horse, the comforting atmosphere of the barn, and the beginning of a new day.

At supper, Red and Alex swapped stories about their most memorable horses.

"Pa, it's so good to see you smile," Karl said. Alex smiled more.

"I'm blessed to be here with all of you," Alex said. "Ma, was it you or Keri who made this ham. Don't think I've ever tasted better." The words were barely out of his mouth before Alex began violently coughing. Gran jumped to her feet and was quickly at his side.

"Karl, bring me a hot cloth. I'm taking your pa to his room." Gran helped Alex stand and begin moving toward the bedroom. The coughing finally ebbed, leaving Alex slumped against the headboard, the quilt bunched at his waist. Gran pressed a damp cloth to his brow and the warm one to his chest, murmuring low and steady like she was gentling a colt. Keri hovered in the doorway, hands twisted in her apron, the lamplight catching the wet shine in her eyes.

Gran glanced back. "Give us a minute, child."

Keri stepped into the hall, but the door stayed cracked. She could hear the soft rustle of sheets, Gran's voice dropping to a whisper that carried anyway.

"Easy, Alex. Breathe with me now… in through the nose, slow as Sunday."

Silence stretched, broken only by the tick of the hall clock. Keri pressed her spine to the wall, feeling every thump of her heart. Soon, Gran emerged from the room and slipped her arm around Keri's waist. "He's finally settled, I think. At least he's not coughing. One of us can check on him later."

The last of the dishes were done as the house hushed to a low ember-glow. Keri stood at the kitchen window, one palm flat against the cool pane, moonlight spilling silver across the barn roof and the pasture beyond. The world outside looked carved from glass—still, sharp, breakable.

Inside her chest, the same brittle ache.

Alex's cough still echoed in the hallway, a ragged ghost that refused to settle. She could see his door from here, the thin blade of lamplight beneath it.

71

Lord, she whispered, the word more breath than prayer. *What can be done? He must feel so helpless.*

The moonlight answered first—no voice, just a hush that pressed against her chest. Then the word rose, gentle as a hand on her shoulder: *pray.* Not a shout. Not a command. Just a quiet, certain, "Pray," the way her pa used to say "Breathe," when she'd fallen and knocked the wind from herself.

Keri closed her eyes. It was clear that Alex was filled with anxiety and pain. Tears slipped, hot against her cool cheeks. *He's afraid, Lord. Afraid there's no room for an old rancher with calloused hands, a fractured faith, and a painful secret.*

Another word drifted up, soft as thistle-down: *Peace.* Not the absence of coughing. Not the absence of pain. A deeper thing—*be still and know.*

She saw it then: Alex in the hay mow someday, lungs whole, laughing as he tossed bales to boys who never tired. Gran beside him, young again, apron gone, hair unbound. Her pa leaning on a pitchfork, grinning like he used to when the harvest was in and the sky was wide open.

No more night. No more coughing. Just morning. Keri pressed her forehead to the glass. The cold bit, but she stayed. *Teach me to pray through this, Jesus. Not past the pain—through it. Give him the kind of peace that comes now, in the midst of pain, and doesn't have to wait for heaven to start.*

The moonlight shifted, a cloud sliding free, and the barn roof suddenly blazed bright, as if the stars themselves leaned down to listen. Keri made her way carefully to Alex's bedroom, peering silently into the door that sat slightly ajar. Her eyes grew wide as they met Alex's wide-awake gaze. He motioned for her to come in. Effortlessly, she moved to his bedside. The lamp had burned low, its wick trimmed to a soft gold coin of light. Alex lay propped on two pillows, the quilt tucked high under his arms, his breathing shallow but steady. Keri sat on the cane-bottom chair beside the bed, her hands folded quietly in her lap, the way her pa taught her when words felt too heavy to hold.

"You shouldn't talk," she cautioned. Alex closed his eyes and shook his head. Alex's eyes, fever-bright, found hers. He lifted one hand—slow, deliberate—and rested it over her clasped fingers. The skin was paper-thin, veins like blue rivers under frost.

"Keri-girl," he rasped, voice scraped raw, "I'm glad God brought you into my life. Glad Karl's got you for a wife. A man couldn't ask for better."

Keri's throat closed. She turned her hand palm-up beneath his, cradling

72

the weight of it. "God doesn't do anything by accident, Alex," she said, soft as the quilt's worn flannel.

"I want you to know—I see your heart, your pa's heart, in that barn, the horses." Alex paused, closing his eyes and catching his breath. "I wish I had known him—your pa."

"He would have liked you, Alex." Eyes moistening, Keri searched her heart to find just the right words to express her thoughts. "Someday, we can all enjoy each other together in heaven. We won't have to worry about being sick or growing old."

Alex grew very somber at her words. "I hope you're right."

"I know I'm right," she whispered, a slight frown wrinkling her forehead. "All we do to get to heaven is believe in Jesus."

Alex eyed her suspiciously. "You're certain?" Keri nodded.

"There's no need to worry, Alex. The Bible says so." Alex reached for her hand, squeezing it gently.

"I'm glad God brought you into my life, that Karl has you for a wife." He had barely finished his sentence when a coughing spell came on again. Keri held onto his hand as he struggled to regain his breath.

"Alex, maybe you have something I need, and I have something you need."

He blinked, slowly. "Reckon that's so?" Alex's breathing came in soft, measured sips; the coughing had passed, leaving only the quiet and the scent of liniment on the quilt. Keri sat close, elbows on her knees, watching the rise and fall of his chest like she was counting blessings instead of breaths.

Her voice was low, the way you speak in church when the sermon's done, and the truth is still settling.

"Having you here, Alex... it's like God reached back and gave me a few more mornings with Pa." Her fingers worried the edge of the quilt, smoothing a wrinkle that wasn't there. "The way you talk about hay crops and horse liniment, the way you look at the barn like it's a living thing; every moment, every word's a real gift."

Alex didn't answer right away. He studied her—really studied—the lamplight catching the damp in her eyes, the faint freckles across her nose, the set of her mouth that was half smile, half ache. Minutes passed, or maybe only heartbeats; in the stillness they felt the same.

At last, he shifted, wincing a little, and found her gaze again.

"And you, Keri," he said, voice rough as river stone, "you're giving me

73

something I can't quite put my finger on. Something . . ."

Keri leaned in, close enough to see the silver in his stubble, the tremor in his lower lip. She whispered it like a secret meant for heaven's ear alone.

"Maybe it's grace?"

The word hung between them, soft as thistle-down, bright as the moon beyond the window. Alex's eyes widened, then softened, the way frost melts under first sun. A tear slipped free, but he didn't blink it away.

"Grace," he repeated, tasting it. "Reckon that's the name for it." He closed his eyes. When he opened them again, any hint of suspicion was gone, replaced by something softer than sleep.

"I reckon," he said, "we're both richer than we knew."

Keri's hand found his, calluses against calluses, two lifetimes of honest work pressed palm to palm. Neither spoke again. Outside, a horse nickered once in the barn, a low, contented sound, as if the night itself had heard and understood. The moon climbed higher, laying a silver bar across the bed like a silent witness. Neither of them moved to break the clasp of their hands.

CHAPTER SIX

Revelations of Grace

The house was dark except for the thin seam of lamplight under Alex's door and the low ember-glow of the stove in the kitchen. Keri quietly made her way up the stairs and eased the bedroom door open, the latch clicking soft as a heartbeat as she closed it. Karl lay on his side, one arm flung across her pillow, breathing deep and even. Moonlight through the window painted silver across the quilt and the strong line of his shoulder.

He stirred when the mattress dipped. "Keri?" A sleepy murmur, thick with dreams. "Pa alright?"

She slipped off her shoes, let her dress fall in a quiet heap, and slid beneath the covers in her shift. The sheets were still warm from his body. "It's something we'll have to talk about," she whispered. "Maybe morning would be better."

Karl pushed up on an elbow, hair tousled, eyes blinking awake. "No. I think we should talk now. I'll be fine." He rubbed a hand over his face. "I don't hear any more coughing. Is he able to sleep?"

Keri turned toward him, cheek against the pillow they shared. "I believe it wasn't the cough so much as a broken heart keeping him awake." Her voice cracked on the last word.

Karl's arm came around her without hesitation, drawing her in until her forehead rested against his collarbone. She could feel the steady drum of his heart under her palm.

"Tell me," he said, lips brushing her hair.

Softly, in halting sentences, Keri shared her conversation with Alex. When she finished, Karl's arms tightened, and she let the tears come, quiet against his nightshirt.

"He's afraid he won't go to heaven," she murmured. "Has he always been like that?"

Karl was silent for a long moment. She felt him swallow.

75

"For as long as I can remember, Pa's been angry," he said at last. "I always reckoned it had something to do with losing Ma, but never really knew what it was about. It sat between us like an impassable canyon when I was growing up. Came between him and most folks, truth be told. Like he was holding the world at bay, afraid to let anyone close enough to see the cracks."

Keri's fingers curled against his chest. "The little black book he reads sometimes—and hides like he doesn't want anyone else to see it. Do you know it?"

Karl shook his head. "Never saw it. Journal, maybe? Not a Bible; he'd have said." A pause. "We'll have to ask Gran in the morning."

Keri nodded, then lifted her face. "We need to pray that he gets past his fear, that God allows us to understand whatever's got such a hold on him."

Karl shifted, sitting up fully now, drawing her with him so they knelt together in the tangle of quilts, knees touching, hands clasped. The moon lit their bent heads like a quiet benediction.

Karl began, voice low and steady. "Father, wrap Pa in your arms tonight. Let him feel the peace that we only find in you . . ."

Keri's turn came soft, trembling. "Show him the door's open, Lord. That grace isn't earned with perfect hands or perfect hearts. Help him let go of whatever is hurting him so."

They prayed until the words ran out and only breath remained. Karl ended it, forehead against hers.

"Thank You, God, for bringing Keri into my life. We're good for each other; Lord, you know it. We've got much to learn, much to share. Help us work together at everything; but especially help us walk Pa through this illness and this heartache. Amen."

He eased them both down, tucking her close, her back to his chest, his arm a shelter across her waist. Outside, the barn roof gleamed creamy-white under the moon, holding its secrets and its horses and the faint, hopeful echo of a cough that had finally stilled.

The first pale threads of dawn slipped through the lace curtains of Alex's bedroom window, painting the walls in soft grays and golds. A cool breath of early autumn air carried the scent of dew-kissed grass and fading roses from the garden below. The house was still, wrapped in the hush of predawn, when a raw, anguished cry shattered the quiet, followed by broken sobs that tore through the walls like a blade.

Karl jolted awake, heart pounding, his bare feet hitting the cold hardwood before his mind caught up. "It's Pa!" he shouted, voice thick with alarm, already halfway out the bedroom door. Keri, startled from sleep, scrambled after him, her nightgown tangling around her legs as they raced down the creaking stairs. The air grew heavier with each step, the faint chill of the morning seeping into their bones.

By the time Keri reached Alex's room, Karl was on his knees beside the bed, gripping his father's trembling arms. Alex thrashed beneath the quilt, his face pale and slick with sweat, eyes squeezed shut against some unseen terror. "Pa, it's all right. I'm here. You're okay," Karl murmured, his voice a low, steady anchor in the storm of Alex's cries. Gran stood behind him, her frail hand resting lightly on Karl's shoulder, echoing his words with a calm that belied the worry in her eyes. "You're okay, Alex. You're safe."

Keri's breath caught as she crossed the threshold, the sight of her father-in-law—usually so stoic, so unbreakable—reduced to a frightened child twisting her heart. She sank to her knees on the opposite side of the bed, the worn rug soft beneath her. The shouting had stirred a violent coughing fit in Alex, his thin frame shaking with each ragged hack. Keri reached out, her hand hovering over his before settling gently on the quilt, afraid to startle him further.

When the coughing finally subsided, Alex's chest heaved, and he blinked into the dim light, his eyes wide and glassy, like a lost boy searching for home. Karl leaned closer, his voice soft but urgent. "Pa, what was it? What scared you so bad?"

Alex's gaze flickered to Karl's face, studying the familiar lines of his son's brow, the worry etched deep. Then his eyes found Keri's, searching for something—reassurance, perhaps, or forgiveness. Her heart ached at the vulnerability she saw there, so raw it felt like trespassing to witness it. Slowly, Alex's gaze dropped to the quilt, his fingers twisting the fabric. "I don't know," he whispered, the words mournful, heavy with something unspoken.

Keri glanced at Karl, their eyes meeting over the bed in a silent conversation. He's not telling the truth, their shared look said. He's carrying something too heavy to name. The weight of it hung in the air, thicker than the dawn mist outside.

Gran's hand tightened briefly on Karl's shoulder, a gentle signal. Karl eased back, giving her space as she shuffled forward and settled into the worn chair beside the bed. The chair creaked softly, a familiar sound in the quiet room. Gran leaned forward, her silver hair catching the faint light, her voice as warm as the first sip of coffee on a cold morning. "Alex," she said, her tone tender but unwavering, "there's something tearing at your heart. We've all seen it these past days. You don't have to carry it alone. Whatever's weighing on you, we're here. We want to help, but we can't if you shut us out."

Alex's eyes stayed fixed on the quilt, his jaw tight, as if meeting anyone's gaze might unravel him completely. "It's nothing," he said, voice barely above a whisper. "I'm fine. Just… some kind of bad dream."

His persistent denial settled over the room like a pall. Keri's chest tightened, her fingers itching to reach for his hand, to promise him he didn't have to face this alone. But she held back, sensing it wasn't time to press in. Outside, a single bird voiced some mournful notes, its fragile sound threading through the open window, a reminder of the world waking beyond these walls.

Gran's lips pressed into a soft line, undeterred. "I'll sit with you a while, Alex. Just to be sure you're settled."

"No need for that," he said quickly, too quickly, his voice cracking like thin ice.

But Gran only smiled, small and stubborn, and folded her hands in her lap. "Humor an old woman," she said. "I'm not going anywhere."

The room fell quiet, save for the distant chirping of the bird and the soft rustling of drying leaves in the morning breeze. Alex's breathing slowed, but his hands still clutched the quilt, knuckles white. Keri and Karl lingered a moment longer, their presence a silent vow: "We're here. Whenever you're ready, Pa."

Keri and Karl climbed the stairs in silence, the pine boards creaking softly beneath their bare feet. The hallway was still dim, lit only by the faint glow of dawn seeping through the curtains. They slipped into their bedroom and sat side by side on the edge of the unmade bed, the quilt rumpled from their abrupt departure. Keri reached for Karl's hands, her fingers cool and steady as they wrapped around his. "What do you think it is?" she asked, her voice low, almost a whisper, as if speaking too loudly might disturb the fragile peace of the house.

Karl shook his head, his gaze drifting to the window where the first blush of morning painted the sky in delicate pinks and golds. The light caught the edges of the maple leaves outside, turning them translucent, like stained glass. He stared for a long moment, then shook his head again, slower this time, the weight of his father's sorrow pressing heavily on his shoulders. "I have no idea what could be such a burden," he said, his voice rough with frustration and love. "I've thought about it over and over. It makes no sense."

Keri studied his face—the tight line of his jaw, the furrow between his brows—and her heart ached for the man she loved, caught between his father's pain and his own helplessness. She squeezed his hands gently. "I think you should ask him about the little black book."

Karl's eyebrows lifted, surprise flickering across his face. He turned the idea over in his mind, the weight of it settling like a stone. "Let's ask Gran about it first," he said finally. "We might as well make some breakfast. There won't be any more sleep now."

"I agree," Keri said, her voice soft but resolute. She paused, then added, "Let's pray first."

Karl bowed his head, his hands still clasped in hers. His voice, when he spoke, was steady but thick with emotion, each word a plea. "Lord, wrap Pa in your comfort. Ease the ache in his heart. Give us wisdom to know how to help him, and bring resolution to whatever's grieving him. We trust you to carry us through. Amen."

They lingered a moment, the prayer settling over them like a warm blanket. Then they rose, dressed in the quiet of the room, and made their way to the kitchen. The room bathed in the gentle glow of morning, the large kitchen window above the sink framed a view of the garden where dew clung to the last of summer's blooms. The air carried the faint sweetness of ripening apples from the barrel sitting on the far end of the room, mingling with the earthy scent of coffee grounds left in the percolator from the night before. The pine table, scarred from years of family meals, stood in the center of the room, its surface warmed by a slant of sunlight. A braided rug, its colors softened by time, lay beneath, and the old cast-iron stove ticked softly as it cooled from the night's embers. Jars of preserves lined the shelves, their ruby and amber contents glinting like jewels in the dawn.

Red slipped through the door and poured himself a cup of coffee as Keri began preparing breakfast. She moved with quiet purpose, cracking eggs into a skillet, the sizzle a comforting sound in the stillness. The ham followed, its savory aroma curling through the room, wrapping the space in warmth.

79

Karl set out plates, his movements deliberate, his mind still turning over the mystery of the black book and Alex's grief. As Keri placed the steaming platters of ham and eggs on the table, Gran appeared in the doorway, her silver hair loosely pinned, her shawl draped over her shoulders. She moved with the slow grace of age but carried the quiet strength of a woman who had weathered many storms.

"Mornin', Red. Keri, breakfast smells heavenly," Gran said, her voice warm as she settled into her chair at the table.

Red surveyed everyone before speaking. "Seemed like you all were up pretty early this morning." Karl glanced at Keri, then leaned forward, his hands resting on the worn wood. "Pa had a nightmare. Pretty bad one. He was pretty shook."

"Sorry to hear that," Red said. "Do you 'spose it has anything to do with whatever has put the burr under his tail?"

"That's what we're thinking, Red. At least he's sleeping right now."

Gran nodded. "For a bit at least, probably till the coughin' gets hold of him again."

Karl cleared his throat and turned to Gran. "Gran, have you ever noticed Pa with a little black book? Something he keeps close, like he doesn't want anyone to see it, maybe?"

Gran's brow furrowed, eyes studying Karl's face as she considered his question. "A little black book?" she repeated, then paused, her lips pressing into a thoughtful line. "Well, come to think of it, your Ma kept a journal toward the last, when she knew her illness wasn't going to get better. I believe it was a little black book."

Karl's heart quickened, a flicker of hope mingling with dread. "What kinds of things did she write about?"

Gran shook her head, her gaze softening with memory. "I never knew," she said quietly. "For the first months after she passed, your father wouldn't let anyone touch a thing of hers. He was . . . so broken. Then one day, he packed up everything—her clothes, her books, all of it—and shipped it to the poorhouse in Cheyenne. He was so bitter about losing her, Karl. I don't know that he kept anything at all."

The words hung in the air, heavy as the morning mist outside. Keri's hand found Karl's under the table, her touch a silent promise: We'll figure this out together. The kitchen, with its familiar smells and sunlit warmth, felt like a sanctuary, yet the shadow of Alex's grief lingered, a puzzle yet to

80

be solved.

The kitchen table fell quiet after Gran's words, the clink of forks against plates the only sound for a moment. Sunlight slid across the oilcloth, warming the last of the coffee in their cups. Keri set her fork down and leaned toward Gran, her voice soft as the morning itself.

"Do you think we should ask him about the journal—if it is a journal, and if he's been reading it?"

Gran folded her hands over her apron, eyes drifting to the window where a single red leaf clung to the pane. She was silent long enough for the percolator to give one last sigh. At last, she spoke, gentle but deliberate.

"Let's pray on it today. I'm not certain it's the best thing to do. I don't want to cause Alex any more grief. He sure seems to have all he can handle right now."

Keri nodded, the worry in her chest easing a fraction at Gran's caution. Karl squeezed her knee beneath the table, then rose to clear the plates. Outside, the sky had lifted to a clear, pale gold; the day was calling them to work.

Karl and Red crossed the dewy yard to the barn, boots leaving dark prints in the grass. The big sliding door stood ajar, exhaling the sweet, familiar perfume of hay and horse. Dust motes drifted in the slanted light like slow golden snow. Four sorrel mares stood in their stalls—Gracie, Pearl, Kate, and Dolly. Their coats gleamed with early-morning brushing, manes rippling like silk ribbons.

Red had already laid out the farrier tools on a folded burlap: nippers, rasp, hoof knife, clinch cutter—each implement worn smooth by years of honest use. Karl haltered Gracie and led her to the tie ring; she nickered, ears flicking forward, trusting the routine. Red ran a calloused hand down her foreleg, lifted the hoof, and cradled it between his knees. The mare stood steady as he pared away the overgrown wall, the rasp whispering in long, even strokes. Shavings curled to the floor like pale wood-petals, scenting the air with warm keratin and earth.

They had just settled into a rhythm—Karl steadying the next hoof, Red trimming with quiet precision—when the barn door creaked wider. Keri stepped through first, sunlight catching the loose strands of her hair, then Alex behind her, moving more slowly, shoulders rounded beneath his flannel shirt. He looked sheepish, avoiding eyes, the nightmare still clinging to him like cobwebs. Karl fetched the short bench from the harness room—dark

81

with saddle soap and age—and set it in the aisle's soft dust. Alex lowered himself gratefully, hat in his lap, and watched the work in silence.

Red glanced up, smiled easy. "Mornin', Alex. Care to keep an old man company?"

Alex managed a nod. His gaze settled on Red's hands—strong, deliberate, yet gentle as they shaped Gracie's hoof. "You learned this from your pa?" he asked, voice ragged from the latest coughs.

Red chuckled warmly. "Every bit of it. Pa was an accomplished horseman—could gentle a bronc with a whisper and a look. Worked beside him till he passed at sixty." He set the rasp aside, picked up the nippers, and clipped a neat quarter inch from the toe. "He was gentle with the horses, but firm. Not a mean bone in him, yet when he spoke, you listened. I was about fifteen when he told me something I never forgot."

He shifted Gracie's weight, cradling the hoof higher so Alex could see the clean, level sole. "Pa said people and horses are a lot alike. 'Red,' he told me, 'you're comin' up on that bridge every soul has to cross. Leads you closer to God, or farther away. It's like this young gelding you're workin'—he don't know you yet, don't trust easy. But he's gotta' decide if he can lean on you before you can do much with him. If he never trusts, you can't ride him, can't ask him to pull his weight. He'll stay wild, maybe even dangerous.'"

Red released Gracie's leg; she set it down with a soft thud and flicked an ear, content. He moved to the offside, voice steady as the rasp's rhythm. "Same with us and the Lord. If we never decide to trust Him, He can't do much for us. We run wild—aren't much use to anyone, might even hurt the ones we love. But once we trust God, we learn to trust others who trust Him, and the world—" He paused, eyes crinkling. "The world becomes a much better place."

Alex listened, motionless. The barn's golden light caught the silver in his hair, the hollow beneath his eyes. A sorrowful shadow crossed his face—deep, private, like a cloud sliding over water. He watched Red's hands shape the hoof into a perfect, balanced cup, but his gaze drifted inward, to some memory only he could see. The rasp whispered on; a horse sighed; somewhere a sparrow darted through the rafters. Alex's fingers tightened on the brim of his hat, knuckles pale, yet he said nothing. The silence that settled was comfortable, respectful, the kind that draws people together.

Karl met Keri's eyes across the aisle. She pressed her lips together, a

82

silent vow to wait, to pray, to love. The morning work went on—hooves trimmed, horses praised with soft words and gentle pats—while the barn itself seemed to breathe around them, warm and alive, holding them all in its wide, sunlit heart.

The supper dishes had been dried and stacked away, the kitchen lamp turned low. Outside, the late fall evening had surrendered to complete darkness; only a thin silver seam of moon edged the barn roof, and the wind moved gently through the cottonwoods, whispering secrets to the night. Keri made her way down the hallway with a candle in a tin holder, its small flame trembling against the draft that slipped under the doors. Shadows danced along the wallpaper—faded roses and vines—until she reached Alex's room. The door stood ajar, a ribbon of lamplight spilling onto the hall runner.

Inside, Alex sat propped against the headboard, quilt drawn to his waist. The little black book lay open on his knee, his thumb tracing a line of ink as though the words might vanish if he blinked. The moment he saw Keri, the book disappeared beneath the quilt with a soft slap of leather on cotton. He folded his hands in his lap and stared toward the window, where the moon painted a pale rectangle on the floorboards.

Keri's heart lurched—half curiosity, half compassion. Before caution could catch her, the words tumbled out.

"Alex, if you'll excuse me for saying so, I've seen you reading that little book several times. Is it a Bible?"

The air in the room seemed to compress. Alex's eyes, usually soft with fatigue, hardened like winter ice on the creek.

"Keri," he said, each syllable deliberate, "I've taken a likin' to you 'cause you're a very likable person. But there are some things that have to remain private. If you'll excuse me for sayin' so, it's really none of your business."

Heat flooded Keri's cheeks; she felt it rise from her collar to the roots of her hair. "I'm sorry," she whispered, stepping back until her shoulders met the door frame. "Truly. If you need anything—anything at all—please let us know. We all care about you very much, you know."

Alex's gaze dropped to the quilt's worn patchwork. "I know," he muttered, the words flat, almost lost beneath the tick of the hall clock.

Keri's throat tightened. She took one small step forward, voice trembling with earnest love. "But not as much as God loves you, Alex. He loves you more than anyone else ever could."

Alex turned his face to the window. A sound escaped him—low, guttural, unintelligible.

"I'm sorry," Keri said softly, "I didn't hear you."

"It's nothin'," he repeated, sharper now. "Nothin'."

The rebuke stung, yet beneath it Keri heard the raw edge of pain, like a splinter too deep to pull. She backed into the hall, candle wavering, and closed the door with the gentlest click.

Every room in the house had settled into night stillness; only the faint scent of woodsmoke lingered from the dying kitchen stove. Keri found Karl already in their room, lamplight gilding the planes of his face as he unbuttoned his shirt. She set the candle on the dresser and sank onto the bed's edge, shoulders folded inward.

"Pa's ok?" Karl slipped in to sit beside her. She studied his face, a rush of regretful heat rising inside her again. She turned to face him. "I asked him about the book," she confessed, voice small. "I shouldn't have. He was . . . sharp with me."

Karl's hands paused; a flicker of exasperation crossed his eyes, and a deep sigh escaped him before he slipped his arm around her waist and drew her against his chest. The flannel of his shirt was warm from the day, smelling faintly of hay and horses and the honest work of his hands.

"It's all right," he murmured into her hair. "I know you meant well." His arms tightened, steadying her trembling. "More than likely, Gran will find a way to ask about it, and maybe over this coming week, we'll learn what it's all about. It touches my heart, Keri, that you care about my pa so much."

She pressed her cheek to his heartbeat. "Sometimes it's like God gave me back some time with my own father," she whispered. "I can't stop praying for him, asking God to relieve his pain, especially the pain in his heart. He doesn't seem to have near the faith Gran does, and he doesn't seem to fully understand your commitment to God."

The lamp had burned low, the wick trimmed short so it wouldn't smoke. Karl and Keri had moved to the bench by the window, close enough that their shoulders touched. Outside, the wind worried the corners of the house, but inside the room felt hushed, almost expectant.

Keri rested her hands in her lap, fingers twisted together. She smiled, small and rueful, then shook her head.

"I don't think I will ever understand God or the Bible the way you do, Karl. You have some kind of… connection I can't even name."

84

Karl's mouth curved, gentle, remembering. "You sound like me after James died."

She turned toward him fully, the lamplight catching the hope and uncertainty in her eyes.

"Those first days," he went on, voice low, "I felt God calling my name every minute—when I was branding calves, when I was eating, when I lay on my bedroll staring at stars that suddenly felt too close. I was confused, even angry. What could God possibly want with a greenhorn cowboy who'd spent years mocking every time James opened his Bible? I'd laughed at him, Keri. Refused to even touch the thing."

Keri's eyes were fastened on him now, wide and steady.

"So, what changed?" she whispered.

Karl looked down at their joined hands. "One night the grief hit so hard sleep wouldn't come for anything. I was bone-tired, heart-sore, and finally I just threw it out there, half challenge, half plea. I said, 'All right, God. I don't know if any of this is real. I don't know if I could ever trust you the way James did. But if you want me—if it's true you've got a plan just for my life—then I'm listening. I'm done running.'"

He lifted his gaze to hers again. "That was it. No lightning. No choir of angels. Just me, a lonesome fire, and a stubborn silence."

Keri's brow creased in surprise. "So this... connection you have now, it didn't come right away?"

Karl shook his head, smiling softly. "Not even close. For weeks, I felt nothing but empty. But I kept listening—reading the little Testament James had left me, watching for signs. And slowly, so slowly I almost missed it, I started hearing him. In a verse that leaped off the page. In the way the sunrise hit the hills just so. In Gran humming an old hymn while she churned butter. He was everywhere, Keri, once I stopped demanding he show up."

He reached out and tucked a stray curl behind her ear. "And you will too. I already see it—you're turning to Him with everything, every time you have a need. That's all he's ever wanted from any of us."

Keri's eyes glistened.

"I believe Pa's still grieving Ma," Karl said quietly. "All that anger, that sharp edge he carries—it's aimed at God, but it spills onto us. Whatever's tearing him up inside, we won't let it come between you and me."

He brushed the curl from her forehead again, letting his fingers linger against her cheek. "And maybe—just maybe—walking through this valley

85

with Pa is the very thing God will use years from now when we're standing in front of our own congregation, helping some other broken soul find the road home."

Keri's breath caught, a soft, wondering sound. "Our congregation?"

The words trembled with warmth, with promise.

Karl's smile was tender, certain, deep as a well and bright as dawn. "Yes, ours. We're one, Keri. I may carry the title someday, the legal duty to shepherd God's flock, but I couldn't be the man God has called me to be without you beside me. You are my helpmeet, my joy, my better and braver half." His voice dropped to a murmur meant only for her. "You mean all the world to me."

For a long moment, she simply looked at him, eyes shining with that rare, settled light—peace and joy braided together so tightly neither the coming journey nor the grief in the next room could unravel it.

Then she leaned forward and rested her forehead against his.

"Together," she whispered.

"Together," he answered, and the word felt like a vow renewed in the quiet lamplight.

CHAPTER SIX

Threads of Redemption

The harvest moon hung low and creamy-gold, so bright it bleached the color from the quilt and laid a silver path across the pine floorboards. Keri woke with a start, heart hammering against her ribs as if it meant to break free. For one breathless second, the house felt suspended, every familiar creak and sigh held in perfect stillness. Then the sound came again—raw, broken sobbing threaded with Gran's low, steady murmur: "Alex, it's all right. You can tell me what's tearing your heart out. Please don't try to carry this alone anymore."

Karl was already swinging his legs over the side of the bed, bare feet hitting the cold floor with a soft thud. Wordless, they moved together down the narrow staircase, the old wood warm beneath their palms despite the midnight chill that seeped through the walls. A kerosene lamp flickered on Alex's bedside table, its flame trembling in a glass chimney etched with soot, throwing wavering shadows that danced like restless spirits across the pine log walls.

Alex lay twisted in the sheets, face contorted, each sob wrenched from a place deeper than lungs. Coughs rattled in his chest, thin and wet, shaking his frame as a wind would rattle dry cornstalks. Gran sat on the edge of the bed in her faded flannel nightgown, one gnarled hand pressed to his back, circling slow and sure, the way she once soothed colts in the barn. The room smelled of camphor, and the faint sweetness of the dried lavender she kept in a tin on the dresser.

Karl and Keri hovered, useless for a moment, then found their places—Karl sinking to one knee beside the bed, Keri pulling the spindle-back chair close enough that its legs scraped softly against the braided rug. The lamp's glow caught the tears on Alex's cheeks, turning them to liquid gold.

After an eternity measured in ragged breaths, the storm inside him eased. He collapsed against the pillows, spent, the quilt bunched beneath his chin

87

like a child's. Gran never moved her hand. Karl reached out, palm open to cover Alex's hand. "Pa," he said, voice low, steady as a ticking clock. "It's time."

Alex's head dipped, a slow, defeated nod. "Yes. I know. I just . . ." His eyes, red-rimmed and aged, lifted to Karl, then to Gran, then Keri. "Please don't hate me." The desperate plea pierced Keri's heart, drawing her closer to the bed and Karl.

Alex reached for Karl's hand, fingers scorched with fever, trembling. He glanced between them as though memorizing faces he feared losing. "It's James." The name came out in a whisper, a prayer, a wound. "Karl . . . James was your brother. Your half-brother."

The silence that followed was thick enough to touch. Outside, a barn owl called once, mournful, then nothing. The lamp flame straightened, steadying.

Karl's lips parted, but no sound came. Gran's hand stilled on Alex's back. Keri felt the room tilt, the way it does when you stand too quickly after kneeling in the garden.

"Pa," Karl finally managed, "what are you talking about?"

Alex withdrew into himself, arms crossing tight over his chest as if to hold the pieces together. "When your ma was so sick . . . I was angry, lonely. Everybody knew it. Didn't want to lose her, didn't want to leave the ranch." His voice frayed. "I was afraid I'd lose everything. No one even wanted to be around me."

Karl leaned closer, the floorboard creaking under his knee. "Pa, no one faults you for hurting when someone you loved was so ill."

Alex's laugh was a broken thing. "If only that were the worst of it." Tears slid into the hollows of his cheeks. "Towards the end, your ma was in the hospital about six weeks or so. I was taking care of everything at the house, the barn, the cattle. One morning, I was at the general store." His gaze drifted to the window, where moonlight silvered the touch of frost on the panes. "That's where I met Sarah."

The name hung soft as moth wings. "She was a new teacher. Pretty. Alone. Like me." He swallowed hard. "I asked her to lunch at the hotel. Don't know what possessed me. I don't know why she said yes. We both knew it was wrong, but..." A shudder. "We saw each other several times a week. Then, three, maybe four times, we were together. My conscience finally got the best of me, and I knew that I was doing wrong by your ma

88

and Sarah. And then your ma was coming home." Alex paused, drawing in some labored breaths, sinking deeper into his pillows. "I didn't know for weeks that Sarah had left town. Called back home to Kansas, someone said."

His chest hitched. Sobs rose again, quieter now, the sound of a man drowning in shallow water. "I never knew she was with child. With James."

Silence was thick as the truth of Alex's words sank in. The lamp hissed softly. Somewhere in the walls, the house itself seemed to sigh.

Gran was the one who moved first. She slid her arms around Alex's shoulders, pulling him gently until his head rested against her collarbone. The flannel of her nightgown absorbed his tears. Karl's hand found his father's again, grip firm, anchoring. Keri sat very still, hands folded so tightly her knuckles gleamed white in the lamplight, praying without words.

The lamp's flame had settled into a steady heartbeat, its small circle of light pooling over the quilt like warm honey. Outside, the moon had climbed higher, turning the frost on the windowpanes into delicate lace that glittered whenever the wind sighed against the glass. Inside, the silence stretched so long it felt like the whole world was holding its breath.

Gran's hand still rested on Alex's shoulder, thumb moving in slow, absent circles the way she once rubbed salve into a scraped knee. When she spoke, her voice was barely louder than the creaking pine timbers, yet it carried the weight of decades of mercy.

"We are so thankful you've shared what's been tearing at you, Alex." She paused, letting the words settle. "Is it all right if we ask a few questions?"

Alex's nod was slight, almost lost in the folds of the pillow. His eyes, red-rimmed and glassy, flicked to each face as though checking for storm clouds.

Gran leaned closer, the lamplight catching the silver in her braid. "Did James know he was your son?"

The question floated down, gentle as a feather. Alex's answer came slowly, wrapped in fresh grief. "No." A tear slipped free, tracing the groove beside his nose before it soaked into the quilt. "Another piece that breaks my heart clean in two. I didn't know myself until after he was gone. His aunt Julie—she wrote me."

He reached for the handkerchief on the nightstand, fingers trembling. The cloth was worn soft from countless washings, embroidered with a tiny G in one corner—Gran's handiwork. He pressed it to his face, muffling a

89

cough that rattled like dry beans in a tin.

"Sarah passed a couple of years before James," he continued, voice muffled. "I remember him telling us about her, quiet-like, over supper one night. Julie said Sarah only told her on her deathbed. Made her swear not to breathe a word to the boy."

Karl's hand, still clasped around his father's, tightened just enough to feel the fragile bones beneath thin skin. "Pa," he said, soft as the hush of snow, "why did Julie send the letter at all, with both of them gone?"

Alex drew a shaky breath, lifting the quilt an inch. "You'd think maybe she wanted to hurt us." A sob cut him off; he pressed the handkerchief harder. When he could speak again, his words came out wondering, almost awed. "But her letter said she believed God wanted me to know that the boy everyone grieved so hard when he passed was truly part of this family."

The room exhaled. Somewhere in the rafters, a mouse scratched once, then stilled. Keri's chair creaked as she leaned forward, the braided rug bunching beneath her bare feet.

Karl's brow creased, confusion and tenderness braided together. "How did James ever find his way to the ranch?"

Alex lifted his head, pillows rustling. Moonlight spilled across his face, softening the hollows beneath his eyes. "I have to believe God brought him." The words rang simple and sure, like a bell across quiet fields. "No other explanation fits."

Silence folded around them again, but it was different now—less jagged, more like the hush after a lullaby. The lamp flame wavered, sending shadows swaying across the walls.

Alex pushed himself upright against the headboard, the effort costing him a cough he tried to swallow. When it passed, he looked from Gran to Karl to Keri, eyes shining with something fiercer than tears.

"I hope you can forgive me," he whispered. "And pray God does too."

Gran answered first. She cupped his weathered cheek with a palm that smelled faintly of lye soap and cinnamon. "Son," she said, voice trembling yet steady, "the forgiving started the minute you started revealing your heart."

Karl leaned in until their foreheads nearly touched, the way he did when he was small and afraid of thunder. "Pa, we're just glad the secret's out where grace can reach it. What happened was wrong, but it looks to me like God can be using it to draw all of us closer to him."

90

Alex eyed Karl warily.

"You remember, Pa, how much I teased James and mocked him for his faith." Karl paused as Alex slowly nodded. "But as he was dying, he was still talking about God."

"I remember." Alex wiped tears from his cheeks.

"I couldn't get that out of my mind, and finally, I knew I had to surrender my life to God, to let him use my life however he wanted to. God blessed James with incredible faith despite all the sorrow that was part of his life. Now, even after James is gone, God is still using his life." Karl looked around at Gran and Keri. "If it hadn't been for James, I wouldn't have even considered being a pastor. And I would never have come to Dakota Territory." He cast a meaningful glance at Keri, whose eyes grew wide at hearing his words.

"Pa." Karl drew close to his father, tightly holding his hands. "Sin is never right, but God's forgiveness and grace covers it. And now, he's taking something that was broken and wrong to bring beauty and peace to all our lives."

The room seemed to draw one quiet breath and hold it. Finally, Alex lay back on his pillows. "Thank you, Karl."

Gran sat back in her chair for the first time in nearly an hour. "I reckon the sun's going to be pushin' that moon out of the way pretty soon. We should probably all try to rest before day breaks."

Alex sat up straight. "No! Please! Before that, Ma, Karl, you have to help me understand this God thing." Gran frowned slightly.

"God thing? Now, Alex, you know that's no way to talk. Are you askin' how to know God has forgiven you for fallin' into sin?"

Alex closed his eyes and nodded. "Yes, I am." Sorrow registered on his face again. "I need to know God has forgiven me and how I can forgive myself." He shook his head. "Ma, all those times when you tried to talk to me about the Bible and listening to God—I pretended to listen, to understand. But I didn't care then. Now . . ." A deep cough interrupted the comment Alex might have made.

Gran motioned for Karl to take her position on the bed. "Karl, this is a question for a man of the cloth, a duty which you will soon take up. Come, tell your pa what he needs to hear."

Karl held up his hand. "Just one minute. I need my Bible."

"Mine is closer," Gran offered.

91

"No, it has to be mine. You'll see why." A few moments later, Karl held the Bible in his hands, the back cover opened to reveal handwritten words on the white page.

"Pa," he began, voice low and steady, the kind that carried across a crowded sanctuary without ever rising to a shout, "James wrote this in his Bible, which I kept after his passing. So, in some way, these are his words to you. You're asking the two hardest questions any of us can ask. Here's what James wrote about the first one: How do I know for certain God has forgiven me?"

Karl leaned forward, lamplight painting golden streaks in his dark hair. "Scripture doesn't leave us guessing. 1 John 1:9 is plain as daylight: 'If we confess our sins, He is faithful and just to forgive us our sins and to cleanse us from all unrighteousness.' That word all doesn't shrink back from the size of what we've done. When we lay our sin bare before God and our family, that's confession. This promise isn't maybe—it's faithful and just. God's justice demanded payment; Jesus made it on the cross. When you trust that payment, the ledger's wiped clean. Not because you feel it yet, but because He is faithful."

Karl paused, letting the words breathe and the idea that, in some sense, James was speaking to them all. Outside, a late-autumn breeze rattled the windowpane, but inside the room felt warmer, as though the stove downstairs had suddenly remembered its purpose.

"Now the second part." Karl read on. "Learning to forgive yourself— that's where the enemy loves to dig in. He'll whisper, 'Sure, God forgives, but look what you did.' That's a lie dressed up as humility. Forgiving yourself isn't pretending the sin didn't hurt; it's choosing to believe God's verdict over your own accusation."

Karl turned to Keri. "Would you collect a small, smooth stone out by the porch and bring it here?" She scurried to gather the stone, returning quickly with a small rock, like one that might be found polished by the water in a creek bed. "Hold this." Karl pressed it into Alex's palm and read on. "It was David who used a stone to defeat God's enemies and God instructs us to "look to the rock" when we need a firm foundation. Every time the shame rises, recognize it as an enemy, grip that stone and say out loud, 'God says I'm forgiven. I will not argue with the Judge.' Say it until your heart catches up with your mouth. Feelings follow obedience, not the other way round."

Alex's fingers closed around the cool weight. A tear slipped, but his shoulders lifted a fraction. "How did he know all that?" he breathed. All four were silent for a few moments as the balm of James' written words sank into their souls.

"I don't think we'll ever know, Pa. But thank God that he did."

Keri touched Karl's arm. "Karl," she whispered. "The little black book?" Karl slipped his arm around her waist and looked to Alex.

"Yes, Pa. Can you tell us about the little black book?"

Alex squeezed his eyes shut and shook his head as one last shard of pain pricked his heart. He reached under his pillow and pulled it out. It measured just four inches wide and six inches tall. The pages inside it made the book just over an inch wide. Alex held it with both hands for a moment before speaking.

"It was your ma's diary, Karl. She started keeping it when she first took sick. The doctors couldn't decide what ailed her, so they wanted her to write down her symptoms every day." Alex looked over toward the window, where the first streaks of morning light were now pushing up over the horizon. "After she passed, I felt so guilty about what I had done, how I had betrayed her. I had a dream—a nightmare—that she knew about Sarah. I thought maybe, if she had found out, she would have written something about it in her diary." Alex paused to clear the rattle in his lungs. "I've read it over and over, nearly every day since I took ill." He shook his head, holding up the book as tears rolled again. "There's not one cross word in here. All she wrote was how much she loved me and you, Gran and Pa, and how sad she was to think that the Lord might take her home."

A new hush settled on them all as Alex finished talking and sank back into the pillows.

"Oh, Alex," Gran said, taking his hand. "I'm so sorry you've had to go through all of this. I know Laura meant every word she wrote in that diary. And I have to believe that, if she were standing here with us, she would say the same thing we're telling you: God has forgiven all of us for all our wrongdoings. It's clear you recognize the error of your ways. She wouldn't want you to always live under the weight of guilt."

"Gran's right, Pa," Karl said, his voice softening. "Look at your family in this room. We've all been praying for you, asking God to help us understand and comfort you. That's a picture of the Father's heart. And now he's answered those prayers. We can be sure, as his word tells us, every morning he has new mercy and grace to cover us for the day."

Gran softly squeezed Alex's hand. "You don't have to feel forgiven to be forgiven. You just have to keep walking in the light you've been given. The rest follows, one sunrise at a time. And speakin' of sunrise, it's nearly here."

Keri jumped up and stood next to Karl. "Gran, you stay with Alex. Karl and I will make breakfast. Red will be in soon, and he'll want his coffee. Alex, we won't say anything to Red."

"You should," Alex answered. "I don't need to tell the whole world, but I'm not going to hide this from those close to me. That is, Karl and Gran, if you won't be shamed by what I've done."

Gran grasped Alex's hand again. "Of course not! Don't even think such a thing, am I right Karl?"

Karl rested his hand on Gran's shoulder. "God is faithful and just to forgive our sins when we confess and repent of what we've done. I know now that any of us can fall into sin at any time. From what God has done with all this, working through James to reach all of us, I'd say God never intended that we should hide it. He is using it for good."

Gran stood to her feet again. "I reckon there's no sense trying to sleep anymore this morning. I'll get dressed and start some breakfast."

Keri stepped next to Gran, slipping her arm around her shoulders. "You go ahead and dress, but Karl and I will get dressed and make breakfast. I think it will be best if you stay with Alex and get a little rest before we eat."

Gran smiled and glanced at Karl. "You have a wise wife."

Keri took Karl's hand, saying, "What do you say about cornbread and honey for breakfast, a delicious way to celebrate the healing God is doing in our family?"

"I think Gran was absolutely right about the wisdom of my wife," he answered.

With each step, the weight of what had just been revealed in the past couple of hours settled on Keri. Her heart ached to know and realize the depth of pain Alex had borne alone for so long. Lord, help us give grace, to love as you love us, to offer healing in every word and gesture.

Dawn had only begun to pale the curtains, and the house still held the hush of night. Karl's hand found the small of Keri's back, guiding her up the stairs as though she were the only steady thing left in a world suddenly tilted.

At the landing, he paused outside their bedroom door, fingers lingering on the worn brass knob. Keri turned to him, the lamplight from below

94

catching the sheen of tears she hadn't yet let fall. She cupped his cheek, thumb brushing the stubble that had grown overnight.

"I'm so sorry, Karl," she whispered. "I know how much James meant to you, and now it must feel like you're losing him all over again."

Her words undid Karl. A single tear slipped free, tracing the line of his nose before he caught it with the heel of his hand. He leaned his forehead to hers, breath trembling.

"I always felt like he was my brother. No wonder he became so special to me . . ." Another tear followed the first. Keri's arms slid around his waist, pulling him inside the room. The door clicked shut behind them, sealing the world out. Morning light filtered through lace curtains, soft as forgiveness, laying pale gold across the quilt on the bed.

His voice trembled as he continued. "He never got mad at me or any of us for taunting him. I'll never forget how foolish that was. And he never flinched. One time, he looked at me with those steady eyes and said, 'God's patient, Karl. He'll wait.' His faith changed my life forever when he witnessed to me while he was dying. Now it all means even more."

The bed's iron frame gave a soft creak under his weight as Karl sat down to pull on wool socks. He reached for the hickory chair where his clothes waited, folded neatly by Keri's hands the night before. The wool trousers were stiff with the chill of the early October morning. He shook them once, the sound sharp in the quiet. He slowly buttoned his flannel shirt, starting at the bottom, fingers steady despite the early hour and stressful night. With the top button missing, the hollow of his throat caught the first gray light seeping through the window. His vest settled over his shoulders like an old friend, a familiar, comforting weight. As he pulled his boots on with a practiced tug, he stopped.

"I keep thinking," he said, "how Pa's failure—his sin—has became the very thread God used to stitch us all together. James wasn't a mistake. He was a bright light. And somehow, even in dying, he's still shining." His voice cracked. "I don't think the Lord's finished with him yet. His story's gonna spill out past these walls, past the homestead, into hearts we'll never meet. I feel it, Keri—like a promise breathing in my chest."

She rose then, drawing him up with her. Their foreheads touched again; her hair smelled of woodsmoke and the lavender sachets she tucked in drawers. Karl's hands found the curve of her waist, anchoring himself.

"If it wasn't for James," he murmured, "I would never have come to

95

Yankton. I would never have met you." His voice dropped to a reverent hush. "I can't imagine a single day without you in it, Keri. Not one. For that alone, I'm forever grateful to James."

Her answer was a kiss—soft, lingering, tasting of the sweet ache of gratitude. When they parted, her fingers threaded through his.

"We have to be gentle with Alex," she said. "He's borne so much. I can't imagine the pain of bearing such guilt, and being terrified to share it with your family."

Karl nodded, swallowing hard. "I know what he did was wrong, but I believe his repentance is sincere. And I have to be thankful for all the ways God has already used this."

The kitchen glowed with the golden scent of cornbread rising in the cast-iron oven, its buttery warmth curling through the air, chasing the night's chill from the corners. Red eased through the doorway, shoulders stooped beneath the weight of accumulating dawns, a dented tin cup cradled in his weathered hands. He poured coffee from the enamel pot—black as midnight, steam curling up to kiss the silver in his beard—then settled into the chair that he had claimed as his, the wood creaking a familiar welcome.

"No Gran this morning?" His voice carried the gentle rasp of a man who'd learned to speak softly so as not to wake sleeping children.

Keri turned from the stove, apron tied snug, a stray curl escaping her braid to dance against her cheek. "She'll be here soon," she said, smiling through the weariness that shadowed her eyes. "We all chased a short night."

Red's gaze lingered on her, then slid to Karl. The lines around his eyes deepened, tender with concern. "Another nightmare?"

Karl drew a slow breath, the steam from his own refilled cup trembling between them. "The last one, Lord willing." He lowered himself into the chair opposite Red. "Pa finally unburdened his soul a few hours ago. Told us what's been gnawing at him all these months."

Red's lips parted; the word came out as a hushed, reverent breath. "Hallelujah."

Karl tipped his head toward the narrow hallway, voice dropping to the peaceful stillness reserved for sacred things. "Lamp's still burning under his door. He wants you to know about it all."

Red's brows lifted slowly, wonder softening the sharp edges of his face. His coffee mug halted mid-air, a quiver rattling his cup. "He does?"

Karl leaned in, elbows on the scarred pine table, voice low enough that the crackle of the stove nearly swallowed it. "Says he's done hiding, Red. Done letting darkness have the last word." His eyes, still red-rimmed from the night's vigil, shone with a fierce, quiet joy. "He's ready to step into the light of God's grace, full and free. And we believe—Keri and I both—that the Lord has a plan to use every tear, every silence, every mile of shame to draw people to himself. Pa's story isn't finished. It's just finding its voice."

Karl's last word still hung in the air when the hallway floor creaked. Gran's small, sturdy frame appeared first, her arm threaded gently through Alex's, guiding him with the quiet authority of a woman who had midwifed a fair amount of babies. Alex moved slowly, shoulders curved like a man testing the weight of mercy, yet his eyes carried a new steadiness, the kind dawn gives after the longest night.

"Miss Keri," Gran sang out, voice bright with morning triumph, "that cornbread's calling my name from clear down the hall. Woke me clean out of a dream about angels, and Alex here says it's stirred his hunger for the first time in weeks." She eased Alex into the chair Red had already pulled out, her palm lingering on his back as if to say, Steady now, you're home. "We couldn't miss the celebration, nor the honey, mind you."

A shy grin tugged at Alex's mouth, the first Keri had seen for days. She crossed the room in three quick steps, apron fluttering, and folded him into a hug that smelled of woodsmoke and lavender. His arms came up slow, then fierce, as though afraid the embrace might vanish. When she pulled back, her hands stayed on his shoulders.

"Cornbread's got two minutes left," she said, voice thick with unshed joy.

"Honey's warm on the stove, butter soft as a promise. Every crumb's a celebration of you."

The cornbread had just come out of the oven, golden and steaming in its skillet, when Alex cleared his throat. The sound was slight, almost lost beneath the scrape of chairs and the clink of butter knives, but it stilled the room all the same.

Keri was pouring coffee, her back half-turned, when she felt his gaze. She glanced over her shoulder and found him watching her, hands folded tight in his lap, knuckles pale.

"Keri-girl," he began, voice rough as if the words had been carried a long way. He swallowed, tried again. "I been thinkin' on somethin'. And if it's too bold, you tell me straight, and I'll hush."

97

Gran paused mid-reach for the honey jar. Red's brows lifted, gentle and curious. Karl set his mug down slowly, giving his father the space to speak.

Alex's eyes, bright hazel now and newly soft, never left Keri's face. "You've been callin' me Alex since the day we met, and that's been right and proper. But if . . . if it ever sits easy on your heart, I'd be honored if you'd call me pa." He lifted one hand, palm open, quick to stop any rush of reply. "Not to take the place of the man who raised you—Lord knows I ain't fit for that. Never will be. But if there's ever a day you need a father's ear, or a hand to steady you, or just somebody to pray over your supper . . . I'd count it the highest privilege to stand in that gap."

The kitchen held its breath. A bead of butter melted down the side of the cornbread, slow and golden.

Keri set the coffeepot down with care. She crossed the floor, knelt beside his chair, and took his weathered hand between both of hers. His fingers trembled, then curled gently around hers.

"Pa," she said, the word tasting of honey and woodsmoke and something more profound than tears. "I'd like that very much."

Alex's eyes filled so fast the sunlight blurred in them. He pressed his free hand to his mouth, shoulders shaking once, twice, before he managed a nod. Keri leaned in and laid her cheek against his sleeve, the flannel warm from the stove's glow.

Across the table, Karl's smile broke wide and quiet, the kind that doesn't need words. Gran dabbed at her eyes with the corner of her apron and declared, "Well, now. Reckon this cornbread just got crowned with glory."

The cornbread had been broken and buttered, the honey jar passed again and again, when Alex set his fork down with a soft clink. The kitchen lamp burned steady, its glow pooling gold across the table like spilled mercy. He drew a breath that trembled at the edges, then looked up, eyes shining with something brighter than tears.

"I am so grateful for all of you. I've lived scared for so long," he said, voice low, steady, the way a man speaks when the storm inside has finally passed. "Terrified of what God might do to me before I draw my last breath, and worse, after. Every creak in the night sounded like judgment coming." He paused, fingers tracing the rim of his coffee cup as if it were the edge of a new world. "But now this morning, I'm wonderin' what blessing He's got waiting in the next sunrise. And I want every soul I meet to taste how wide his grace runs, how deep His mercy goes."

His gaze drifted to Red, then to Karl, lingering there. Red's eyes, soft with understanding, flicked to Karl.

"Alex, I'm so grateful to see God healing your heart," Red said. "And I'm wonderin' on somethin'. He leaned forward, elbows on the table. Alex, Karl, what would you say to tellin' your story in church?" He glanced at Karl, then back to Alex. "Not the fall, not the shame. Just the part where God took the broken pieces—James, Karl, all of you—and wove something beautiful. How he pulled us together like broken pieces of a beautiful picture. The truth of grace that don't flinch, forgiveness that don't keep score."

Alex's breath caught. He looked down at his hands, scarred, trembling, then up again, meeting Karl's eyes with a wonder that bordered on reverence. "I can't erase what I did," he whispered. "Lord knows I'd give anything to scrub it clean. But I can lay it down. Give it all to him and let him use it however he sees fit." His voice cracked, soft as breaking dawn. "That's what I want, son. To let him turn my mess into a message."

A tear slipped free, tracing the weathered line of his cheek. He reached across the table, gripped Karl's forearm with fingers that shook but held fast. "I don't have much time left," he said, the words a vow. "A few months, maybe less. But every sunrise, every sunset, I'll be on my knees for you, and Keri, and Ma. Prayin' God keeps you close, keeps you strong, keeps you wrapped in the same grace that's holdin' me now."

Keri's hand found his other arm, her touch light but fierce with love. The kitchen held them all in its warm embrace, the scent of cornbread, the hush of held breath, the quiet certainty that something sacred had just taken root.

CHAPTER EIGHT

A Final Homecoming

The house was never truly dark. A single kerosene lamp burned low on the kitchen table, its flame trembling inside the glass chimney like a heartbeat. Down the hall, another lamp—Gran's bedside one with the cracked rose globe—cast a bruised peach glow across Alex's room. The wind prowled the eaves, rattling the loose shingle above the porch, but inside, time had narrowed to the space between one labored breath and the next.

Karl sat on the floor outside Alex's bedroom door, back against the wall, knees drawn up. His suspenders hung loose; his shirt was unbuttoned at the throat. Every few minutes, he pressed his ear to the wood, listening for the wet, rattling inhale that meant Alex still clung to the earth. When it came, Karl's shoulders loosened a fraction. When it didn't, he counted—one, two, three—until it returned, thin as a thread.

Keri moved like a ghost between kitchen and sickroom, her apron swapped for Gran's old flannel nightgown, sleeves rolled past the elbows. She carried a tin cup of water, a damp cloth, and a spoon. Anything that might buy Alex one more minute of ease. The rising bread she had shaped hours earlier now baked in the oven, its fragrance drifting through the house—warm, yeasty, impossibly hopeful—mingling with the sharper scents of camphor and laudanum.

Gran had not left the rocking chair since dusk. She held Alex's hand in both of hers, thumb tracing the blue veins that stood out like rivers on a map. His fingers were hot, the skin paper-thin. Every so often, she leaned forward and whispered a verse into the shell of his ear, the same ones she had whispered the night he was born, the night the grasshoppers came, the night the mortgage nearly took the ranch.

"The Lord is my shepherd; I shall not want..."

Alex's eyes fluttered. Sometimes they fixed on her face, recognition

100

flickering like a match struck in wind. Sometimes they stared past her, at something the rest of them could not see.

Doc Warner HAD arrived before dawn, his boots caked with frozen mud from the road. He smelled of coal oil and winter air. Karl met him on the porch, took the black bag without a word, and led him down the hall.

Doc's examination was gentle but swift. He pressed the stethoscope to Alex's chest, listened, then lifted his nightshirt to reveal the sharp cage of ribs, the hollow beneath them. Consumption had burned away everything but his stubborn heart and those bright, undefeated eyes.

Gran stood at the foot of the bed, arms wrapped around herself. "Doc?" Her eyes revealed the questions she couldn't voice, wanted to push out of her thoughts. Doc motioned for her to step outside the room.

He removed his spectacles and rubbed the bridge of his nose. "Probably just hours now. Maybe till noon. Use the laudanum freely now. I can't imagine he would rally. Only decline." He returned to Alex's bedside, gave him a comforting pat on the shoulder, then left the brown laudanum bottle on the washstand, beside the basin where Keri wrung out cloths in water gone cold hours ago. Then he was gone, the bedroom door closing soft as a sigh.

Keri stared at the bottle. Freely. The word lodged in her throat like a fish bone.

The first evidence of sunrise was pushing up over the eastern sky as the kitchen lamp burned low, its flame steady in the draftless room. A single square of cornbread, rewarmed on the stove top, sat on a blue willow plate between Keri and Karl. Steam curled from the crumb, carrying the sweet, nutty scent of yesterday's baking. A small crock of sorghum syrup gleamed dark amber in the lamplight, its surface dimpled where Karl had dipped the spoon.

Keri broke the cornbread in two, handed half to Karl. Their fingers brushed—calloused, familiar, trembling just a little. They ate quickly, not because they were hungry, but because Gran was waiting in Alex's room, and the day was slipping away faster than either wanted to measure.

Karl swallowed, wiped his mouth with the back of his hand. "Pa never did like cornbread," he said, his voice rough. "Gran made it a lot, and he ate it, but he didn't enjoy it much."

"What will you remember about him, Karl?"

Karl set the sorghum spoon down, the clink soft against the plate. "You

101

know what I always carried in my pocket when I was knee-high to Pa?" His voice was low, warm with memory. "A little scrap of rawhide he cut from an old trace line. Said it was my 'worry knot.' Any time the world felt too big—blizzard coming, calf born breach—I'd rub that knot between my fingers and remember what he told me the day he gave it over."

Karl's thumb traced an invisible circle in the air, the motion slow and deliberate.

"When I was about 10, I was scared to push cattle when we drove 'em from one pasture to the next. I'd seen a hand on another ranch be gored by a longhorn cow that turned on him when he was pushing a small herd. It was a sight I'll never forget. I was ashamed to be afraid, but Pa told me a man's strength ain't in never being afraid. It's in kneeling down, afraid, and still choosing to do the next right thing. He'd be out before dawn, wind cutting like a skinning knife, checking the herd in nothing but his coat and that quiet certainty. Never raised his voice to the horses, never to us. Just looked you in the eye and you knew the job would get done because he'd already decided it would."

He smiled, small and crooked. "I must've worn that rawhide smooth by the time I was twelve. Still got it tucked in my Bible case."

The kitchen lamp had burned down to a soft gold coin of light, just enough to gild the crumbs on the blue willow plate. Keri rested her elbows on the oilcloth, chin in her hands, watching Karl. The sorghum crock sat forgotten between them; the cornbread was gone, but the sweetness lingered on their tongues and in the hush.

Karl pushed his chair back an inch, the legs scraping like a whisper. He folded his big hands on the table, knuckles scarred from plow handles and barbed wire, and stared at them as if reading a map only he could see.

"You know the one thing about Pa that still sits in my chest like a compass needle?" he began, voice low, steady, the way it got when he spoke of sacred things. "Persistence. Not the loud kind—never hollered, never stomped. Just a quiet, iron refusal to let a job beat him."

He lifted his gaze to Keri, eyes shining in the lamplight. "The spring I was 14, we were losing new calves to wolves left and right. Pa was determined to bring it to a stop, so we packed some supplies, grabbed two hands, and headed out with a tent to the flat where the cattle had gathered."

The early spring weather had been mild for nearly two weeks, Karl explained. Alex was confident that he and the two hands could circle the

102

herd at night to ward off wolves, and that plan seemed to be working for the first two days.

"Would you believe those crafty wolves used a single wolf as a decoy to get Pa and the hands to go after it, then the rest of the pack took out three calves in just minutes?" Karl shook his head. "Pa wasn't deterred one bit. After another day, he sent one of the hands home to help with the chores. That same evening, our picketed horses broke loose, and we never did find one of them. The hired hand was ready to give up and kept telling Pa, 'You can't win this battle.'"

Karl gave a soft huff of laughter, more breath than sound. "Pa didn't argue. Just looked at me—steady, like he was measuring the man I might become—and said, 'Son, can't is a word for folks who quit before they start. Find a way around, through, or over. We're in this together till it's finished."

"What happened with the wolves?" Keri's wide-eyed question made Karl smile.

"Our neighbor got wind of our predicament and sent a hand over with strychnine. Pa recovered a calf carcass, laced it with strychnine, and after one more night, the wolves were gone. They never came back as strong after that year."

Keri smiled. "He won't really be gone, you know. We know where he is."

Karl reached for her hand. "Same place as your pa. In God's presence." He affectionately squeezed her hand. "Same place we're all going one day." He paused to reflect further. "More than once, he told me, 'Son, there's more in you than you think.' I believe that now. I'm glad he wasn't willing to let me settle for less than what I could accomplish."

Keri's eyes traced the traces of pain in his face. "I wish I'd known him longer, but through what you've shared, I feel I know him better."

Keri turned her hand palm-up, laced her fingers through his. "I'm thankful for the iron I see in both of you, and for the tender heart."

Karl squeezed once, gently. "We should go back to his room, so Gran isn't alone too long. If Pa's awake, I want him to know we're all right there with him." They rose together, the chair legs whispering again, and carried the warmth of cornbread and memory down the hall like a lantern against the dark.

The hall smelled of camphor and lavender water and of the beeswax candle Gran kept burning beside the bed. The candle seemed a small effort to purify the room's air, although Doc Warner was skeptical of its purifying

103

effect. However, Gran felt it was one thing she could do for Alex, and Doc didn't disagree. Alex lay beneath the wedding-ring quilt, his chest rising in shallow, even breaths—sleep, not the restless kind, but the deep, still kind that comes when the body has decided to rest, whether the soul is ready or not. It was the third day that sleep had claimed him for nearly 24 hours per day.

Gran sat in the rocker, Bible open on her lap, a shawl around her shoulders. Wisps of her silver hair had come loose from the pins holding the carefully shaped bun. The rebellious hairs framed her face like elegant elements of lace. She looked up as Karl and Keri entered the room, smiled the small, steady smile that had carried all of them through every difficult day and challenge over the past year.

"Sit," she whispered, patting the foot of the bed. "He's been still nigh on an hour. Laudanum's dispensing its blessings."

Keri sank onto the quilt's edge, careful not to jostle the mattress. Karl took the cane-bottom chair opposite Gran, leaning forward, elbows on his knees. The three of them formed a quiet triangle around the frail and fragile man who had once been the family's source of strength and leadership.

Gran opened the Bible to the page marked with a sprig of dried sage. "Psalm 23," she said, and began to read, her voice low and musical, the way she used to read to the children on winter nights when the wind howled like wolves.

"The Lord is my shepherd; I shall not want. He maketh me to lie down in green pastures . . ."

Keri's eyes never left Alex's face. The lamplight painted his cheekbones soft gold, prominent now that his ravaged body was failing. She reached out and brushed a lock of damp hair from his forehead. His skin was warm—too warm—but peaceful.

Gran paused, slipping a small hand-stitched quilt square - no larger than a dinner plate - out of her Bible. "Karl, do you remember this?" She held up the fabric square for Karl and Keri.

"It's the calico from great-grandma's wedding dress," Karl answered, taking the fabric Gran handed to him. "Isn't that a piece of Pa's baby blanket and first chambray shirt?" He turned the fabric over and examined both sides. The stitches were uneven, made of coarse linen thread.

"Your great-grandma made it shortly before she passed. Her hands were already plagued by arthritis when she started it," Gran said. "Her plan was

104

to make a full quilt, but this was the only square she was able to finish. She flattened those saddle nails herself to create that cross, then stitched them to the cloth with the small bit of red thread she had. From what I've been told, she never wasted one scrap of fabric that came her way."

"That was our brand -that single cross and the R." Karl's eyes were wide as he questioned Gran.

"Yes," she answered. "I'm told she finished it the night before she passed away after birthing your grandpa's stillborn sister. Childbed fever, they said." A reverent quiet filled the room for a few moments before Gran continued. "I found it under your pa's pillow this afternoon. He was very close to his grandpa, who used to carry the piece in his Bible. I hadn't seen it for years. He must have had it in the satchel he packed. I reckon it's brought him some comfort in recent days."

The room was quiet but for the soft rasp of Alex's breath and the low crackle of the hearth. A single kerosene lamp burned low on the dresser, its flame trembling inside the glass chimney like a heart that refused to give up. Shadows pooled in the corners, but the firelight caught on the quilt square as Gran gently laid it in Alex's open palm—indigo stars gone silver with age, the tiny red cross at the center glowing like a coal.

Gran sat in the rocker, her hands folded over the apron she'd worn since dawn. Keri perched on the foot of the bed, one hand resting lightly on Alex's ankle beneath the quilt. Karl stood at the window, shoulders rounded, staring out at the snow that had started to fall again—big, slow flakes drifting past the frost-laced pane.

Gran's voice came low, the way wind moves through cottonwoods. "His granddaddy carried that scrap in the front of his Bible for thirty years. Every night he'd open to 2 Corinthians 12:9, 'But he said to me, "My grace is sufficient for you, for my power is made perfect in weakness."' He laid that little scrap of fabric flat on the page, like a bookmark for grace. He never said, but I suspect it made him feel closer to his wife after she passed."

Karl turned from the window. "Pa used to tell that his grandpa let him touch it when he was little. Told Pa it was his grandma's beautiful heart stitched into every thread. Said the cross was part of the ranch brand, but the stars were her dreams for him and all of us."

Gran nodded. "Dreams she never got to see."

Alex stirred then, a small sound catching in his throat. His fingers curled around the quilt square as if it were the only solid thing left in the world. His

105

eyes opened—milky now, but still the same hazel brown-green—and fixed on the scrap. A tear slipped from the corner of one eye. He lifted the square with trembling effort, holding it up to the lamplight. The indigo stars caught the glow and threw it back like distant constellations.

"Happy . . . times," he mouthed, the words barely audible. Gran leaned forward, smoothing a lock of damp hair from his fevered forehead. Keri's hand tightened on his ankle. Karl crossed the room in two strides and dropped to his knees beside the bed.

Alex's gaze found his son's. With what strength remained, he grasped Karl's hand—skin paper-thin, veins like blue rivers under frost—and pressed the quilt square into Karl's palm. The cloth was warm from Alex's grip.

"Legacy," he whispered, voice cracking like thin ice. Tears welled again, spilling faster now. "My legacy . . . not so good. Their legacy . . . " He tapped the quilt square weakly. "Unforgettable."

Karl's throat worked. He folded his fingers over the scrap, pressing it to his chest as if to keep it from flying apart. "Pa," he said, voice thick, "you have a wonderful legacy. I will always remember your strength—how you faced challenge after challenge, the drought, the nights you thought the wolves would take everything, all the years of walking in loneliness. And now, how God is using your life as an illustration of his mercy and grace in the face of your repentance. What better legacy could we have than to know that God welcomes us back to himself when we fall and tells us–as 2 Corinthians 12:9 says, 'my grace is sufficient for you'? You have proven to us that all we really need is God and his grace."

Alex's lips curved—a faint, trembling smile that held every sunrise he'd ever watched from the ranch house porch or a saddle. His eyes fluttered shut, lashes dark against the pallor of his cheeks. The quilt square rose and fell with his shallow breaths, a tiny flag of surrender and triumph both.

Outside, the snow kept falling, soft as forgiveness. Inside, the lamp burned steadily, and the room smelled of woodsmoke, lavender water, and the faint sweetness of beeswax from the candle Gran had lit earlier—an unspoken prayer curling toward the rafters.

Alex slept again, the quilt square cradled between father and son like a covenant older than sorrow.

The room had grown so still that the only sound was the soft, wet labor of Alex's breathing—each inhale a minor, stubborn miracle, each exhale

106

a letting-go. Outside, the November sky hung low and pewter, scattering snow showers that tapped the windowpane like hesitant fingers. The wind, which had moaned all afternoon, eased into silence as Alex's chest rose one final time, then settled.

Gran sat closest to the bed, her gnarled hand resting on Alex's brow, smoothing the damp silver hair as she had when he was a boy with fever. Keri knelt next to Karl, one arm around Karl's waist, the other clasping Gran's shoulder. Karl knelt, Alex's frail fingers folded inside his own—skin to skin, pulse to fading pulse.

They did not speak of goodbye; the word felt too sharp for the hush. Instead, gratitude rose like incense: He is done hurting. Alex's face, once etched with pain, had softened into something almost boyish, the consumptive flush replaced by a waxen peace.

Karl bowed his head. Gran's free hand found his, and Keri's fingers laced through both of theirs—a small, unbreakable circle.

"Heavenly Father," Karl began, voice steady though tears tracked his cheeks, "we thank you that we can be assured Pa is with you right now, rejoicing in heaven because he put all his trust in you these last weeks. There's no pain, no sorrow, no regrets to weigh down his heart. Only the peace and joy that awaits all who trust you with their life. Guide us now as we enter this new season and follow your leading into those good works you have planned for us in the weeks and months ahead."

The prayer drifted upward. As the final "Amen" left their lips, the kerosene lamp gave one last valiant flicker—flame bowing, then surrendering. Darkness folded gently over the room, broken only by a sliver of moonlight that slipped between clouds and danced across the falling snow. Each flake caught the light for an instant, a thousand tiny lanterns escorting Alex home.

Gran leaned forward and pressed her lips to his forehead, a mother's benediction. Keri's sob was soft, almost a laugh of relief. Karl did not let go of the hand that no longer squeezed back; he simply held it, as if to anchor the moment between earth and eternity.

Outside, the snow kept falling—quiet, deliberate, covering the world in a hush deep enough to hear angels sing.

107

CHAPTER NINE

A Prodigal's Legacy

The little white church on the ridge had never been so full. Snow sifted against the steeple like flour through a sieve, and every window glowed amber against the iron-gray morning. Inside, the pot-bellied stove at the back roared, sending waves of cedar-scented heat rolling down the aisle. Pine boughs laced with scarlet bittersweet draped the rafters; someone had tucked a sprig behind each hymn-number board, so the whole sanctuary smelled fresh and bright.

The pews creaked under the weight of the town. Farmers in Sunday suits patched at the elbow stood three deep along the walls, boots dripping meltwater onto the wide-plank floor. Women in deep mourning frocks, black bombazine and wool shawls, filled every inch of bench, handkerchiefs already damp. Children perched on parents' knees, solemn and round-eyed. The coffin, quilt-draped on the bottom half, rested on sawhorses before the pulpit, the pine lid propped up to reveal Alex's body. He looked smaller than any of them remembered, worn down to the pure lines God had first drawn. His face was white as fresh linen, calm as still water at dawn, and the faintest smile touching his lips — the kind of smile a man wears when the pain is finally gone and home is just over the rise. The quilt lent a wealth of warm colors through the feed-sack calico, wedding-ring scraps, and the scarlet Forgiven Gran had stitched on the middle squares at dawn.

Keri sat on the front bench between Gran and the aisle, one arm slipped gently around the older woman's shoulders. Gran's spine was straight as a fence post, but her hands trembled in her lap, twisting the same black handkerchief into knots and then smoothing it out again. Every few minutes, a shudder ran through her, small but deep, like wind rippling wheat. Keri drew her a little closer, pressing Gran's silver head to her own shoulder without a word. Keri's eyes kept drifting to the coffin, then away, then back again, as if she could hold onto Alex a little longer just by looking.

108

Karl stood behind the rough pulpit, Bible open in front of him. His voice was steady, but Keri could hear the places where grief tried to crowd in, and he pushed it back with Scripture the way a man shoulders a gate shut against a storm.

His gaze found Keri's over the heads of the congregation. His coat was brushed, his hair combed, but grief had carved new lines around his eyes. For a heartbeat, the weight of everything (the coffin, the grieving mother beside her, the flock looking to them both for strength) passed between them. Keri lifted her chin the tiniest bit and gave him the same small, steady smile she'd given him during many challenges: I'm here. We're enough. Keep going.

Karl closed the Bible and let the silence settle for a long breath before he began, his voice steady but thick with the weight of love.

"'Let not your heart be troubled,' Jesus said. 'Ye believe in God, believe also in me. In my Father's house are many mansions . . . I go to prepare a place for you.'

"Alex Richmond lived a hard life, and he died a hard death. Consumption took its slow toll, but it never took his story. And the last words he spoke to me, with the rattle already in his chest, weren't about the pain, or the ranch slipping through our fingers, or even about the wife waiting for him on the other side. He gripped my hand, looked me square in the eye, and said, 'Tell 'em all I finally understood grace.'"

A soft rustle moved through the room, heads bowing, hands reaching for hands.

Gran's breath hitched. Keri felt Gran's fingers find hers and squeeze once, hard, as if to say, "He did. He finally did." Keri tightened her arm and turned just enough to murmur against the gray hair at her temple, "He's already there, Gran. He's warm. He's whole. And he's waiting on us."

Gran gave the slightest nod, but the tears came anyway, sliding silently down the deeply creased cheeks. Keri reached into her sleeve, drew out her own handkerchief, and pressed it into Gran's hand.

Red sat on the other side of Keri, his big frame overflowing the narrow bench, shoulders hunched like he was trying to take up less space in a world that suddenly felt too small.

When Karl spoke those last words—"Tell 'em all I finally understood grace"—Red's head came up slowly. His eyes, already red-rimmed from the long night and the long ride, fixed on Karl with something fierce and

109

wondering in them.

Behind them, a baby fussed; its mother hushed it quickly. Someone in the back row coughed, then thought better of it and swallowed the sound.

"That was Pa's victory cry," Karl went on. "You all know the road that brought him there. A wandering cowboy named James—sent by God, though none of us knew it then—riding onto our place with a Bible in his saddlebag and the gospel burning in his heart. James poured out his life sharing Christ with men who laughed at him, and he died before he ever learned he was working with his family. Yet God used even that sorrow, those hard years, that seeming waste, to soften the heart of the father James never recognized.

"Grace protected the fatherless young man. Grace worked through that young man to bring him to his lost father. Grace took a broken, angry, grieving man and made him a bridge so that others—you, me, every soul in this room—could cross over into the same mercy.

"That is the legacy breathing in this room today.

"Pa didn't leave gold or acres. He left a map: one prodigal, one road home, one Father running to meet him. He told his story without varnish: 'I was lost, and He found me.'

A low sound escaped Red, half groan, half laugh, the kind that starts in the boots and rumbles all the way up. He dragged the heel of his hand across his face, not even pretending to hide the wet on his cheeks anymore.

"We know now," Karl continued, voice lifting like a light in the dark, "Pa is in heaven, rejoicing with his Savior. No more cough, no more fever, no regrets to weigh him down. He put all his trust in Jesus, and Jesus kept every promise.

"So today we do not mourn the man the sickness took. We rejoice for the man grace brought home."

Karl stepped down from the pulpit and laid his hand on the wedding-ring quilt folded across the coffin.

"Pa's story isn't finished. It's stitched into every one of you—into every prayer answered, every prodigal welcomed, every wandering heart brought back to the fold. Grace isn't earned; it's received—by anyone, anyone— who comes with empty hands and a repentant heart.

"Pa proved it. And every time we forgive as we have been forgiven, every time we run to meet the wanderer instead of turning away, we keep walking the road our heavenly father marked out for us. We follow the example of our Lord . . . and we honor the legacy of a man who finally understood grace."

He bowed his head.

"Let the church say Amen."

A single, strong "Amen" rose from the congregation, broken and beautiful, and rolled through the little sod church like living thunder.

Karl closed the Bible. "So today we don't mourn the man the sickness took. Rejoice for the man grace brought home."

Around them, the congregation sat wrapped in a hush so deep the only sound was the soft crackle of the stove and the occasional muffled sob. No one wanted to be the first to break the moment when heaven felt close enough to touch.

The final amen still hung in the pine-scented air when the congregation stirred like a sleeper turning toward morning. The pot-bellied stove at the back of the sanctuary crackled and popped, sending up a fresh gust of cedar heat that chased the November chill from coat collars and bombazine sleeves. Snow tapped the frosted windows in soft, persistent Morse—he's home, he's home—while inside, the Ladies' Aid Society moved with the quiet efficiency of women who had buried husbands, babies, and dreams.

Across the aisle from Gran and Keri, Josiah Raskin sat alone, collar turned up, eyes fixed on the coffin. He had come early, paid the undertaker, and now seemed unsure where to put his large, repentant hands.

One by one the congregation—rough-handed men and wool-bonneted women, some who had ridden twenty miles through snow to be there—filed slowly past the open casket where Alex lay in his Sunday coat, hands folded over Gran's wedding-ring quilt.

Old Lars Hansen went first, hat clutched to his chest like a shield. He stopped, looked long, and whispered in Norwegian something that sounded like a prayer and a goodbye all at once. His wife Ingrid laid a small bundle of dried lavender on Alex's breast and gently patted the quilt twice.

The homesteader from up on the ridge, the one who'd lost his own boy to the same sickness, just touched two fingers to the edge of the coffin and nodded once, hard, as if sealing a bargain with heaven.

Mrs. McAllister, who always sat third pew left and sang harmony whether the hymn had one or not, leaned in and said clear enough for the front rows to hear, "Rest easy, Alex. The angels are already jealous of that smile." Then she pressed a handkerchief to her mouth and moved on before

111

the tears spilled.

The cowboys came in a cluster, spurs wrapped in burlap so they wouldn't clink. Young Tommy Rawls (barely seventeen and still growing into his wrists) went fish-belly white, turned quick, and had to be steadied by the man behind him.

And then came Red.

Red stopped square in front of the coffin like a horse that's just seen a rattlesnake. His hat was already crushed hard in his hands. He stared down at Alex a long time. The whole church held its breath. Finally Red reached out one ham-sized hand, slow and careful, and laid it on Alex's folded ones. The freckles stood out stark against the sudden pallor of his face.

"My friend," he said, voice cracking like green wood on a fire, "I'm lookin' forward to all the long talks and celebrations we're gonna' have on the other side. You can show me around, okay?" He swallowed hard enough the sound was audible in the hush.

Red leaned down, pressed his hand on Alex's folded ones for a heartbeat— just a heartbeat—then straightened, swiped his sleeve across his eyes, and stepped aside so the next person could pass.

But he didn't go far. He stood against the wall the rest of the service, arms folded tight, staring at the coffin like he was memorizing it, singing the hymns in a rumble that shook the benches when they finally closed the lid.

When the pallbearers lifted the box, Red was the first to take a shoulder under it, and folks said later his eyes were still wet when they lowered Alex into the frozen ground just outside the church.

Mrs. Hansen and Widow Kline had slipped out during the last hymn; now they returned through the side door, arms laden with quilt-wrapped bundles. A plank table—borrowed from the Sunday school room—appeared as if by sleight of hand, draped in a red-and-white checkered cloth already fragrant with steam. Two graniteware coffeepots the size of milk pails perched on the stove's flat top, their spouts hissing like contented cats. A third pot, carried in by the blacksmith's wife, was wrapped in a crazy-quilt cocoon to keep the coffee scalding.

Gran stood at the head of the table, black dress crisp despite the sleepless night, her silver hair pinned tight beneath a lace cap. She lifted the lid from a basket and the scent of warm gingerbread rose like a benediction—molasses and clove, the same recipe she'd used untold times in her own home.

Keri worked beside her, slicing pound cake with a bone-handled knife.

112

Each wedge was thick as a hymnal, golden at the edges, studded with currants that gleamed like tiny stained-glass windows. She laid them on a pressed-glass platter, its scalloped rim catching the lamplight in soft prisms. She moaned quietly as the knife slipped, creating a crooked piece.

Gran covered her hand and whispered, "No need to worry child. Heaven's got room for crooked cake, too."

The men formed a loose queue, enamelware cups balanced on saucers that doubled as plates. Josiah Raskin hovered at the edge, coat unbuttoned now, the stern lines of his face softened by steam and sorrow. The blacksmith—callused hands gentle as a mother's—pressed a cup into Raskin's grip.

"Good to have you here, Mr. Raskin."

Raskin's throat worked. "Call me Josiah. Never thought I'd stand in this church. Not after—" He couldn't finish. The blacksmith clapped his shoulder and moved on, leaving Raskin clutching the cup like a lifeline.

Children darted between boots and skirts, snatching molasses cookies shaped like stars. One little girl—freckles stark against winter-pale skin—offered her cookie to Gran with grave solemnity.

"For Mr. Alex," she lisped. "So he's not hungry in heaven."

Gran knelt, skirts pooling like spilled ink, and accepted the gift with both hands. "He's feasting, darling. But I know he'd love to have your gift."

Laughter threaded through the low murmur—soft, astonished, the sound of grief discovering it could still breathe. A farmer leaned against the wall, coffee steaming beneath his mustache. Gentle laughter swelled, warm as the potbellied stove, and Karl felt the weight of the day settle in his chest like ballast. He caught Keri's eye across the gingerbread; she lifted a slice in silent toast. He's home, her gaze said. But he will always be with us in some way, until we're all together again.

Gran poured the last cup of coffee, then pressed it into Karl's hands. "Drink, son. Your pa's not the only one who needs strength today."

"Strong enough to float a horseshoe. Must be Pa's recipe." Gran smiled.

Outside, the snow kept falling, erasing wagon tracks, softening the world's sharp edges. Inside, the church smelled of gingerbread and grace, and the quilt on the coffin seemed to glow—every square a life touched, every stitch a prayer answered. Alex Richmond had passed from earth, but the legacy he left was just coming to life.

Josiah Raskin stood near the last pew, hat in his hands, turning it slowly as if the felt brim might unravel if he stopped moving his fingers. The church was almost empty now; only the low murmur of the family and the faint creak of old wood settling back into silence. He had meant to slip out quietly after the final prayer, the way a man leaves a place he has no real claim to, but some unseen force had kept him there as the church emptied. Now Gran was walking toward him with that steady, determined stride that made escape impossible.

"Josiah, thank you for all you did for Alex and for being here today." She extended her hand, which Raskin readily grasped in a handshake. "Tell me, Josiah, where will you have your Thanksgiving meal Thursday?"

Raskin's eyebrows raised slightly. "For the past few years, I've taken dinner at the hotel. It's usually pretty quiet, but that suits me."

"Well, we won't likely have such fancy food as the hotel, but we'd be honored if you'd consent to join us for dinner that day."

Raskin's eyes widened. He attempted to protest, polite and automatic, but his throat closed around the words. The warmth in her voice cracked something loose inside his chest that had been clenched tight since the moment he'd heard Alex was gone.

"That's a lovely invitation, Gran. Are you certain that's what you want?"

Gran moved in closer to him, capturing his eyes with her own. "Josiah, we will both have an empty chair at our tables come this Thursday. I've lived enough years to know that the best way to soothe a heartache is to reach out to someone who knows the same kind of sorrow. You'd be doin' us a favor by sayin' yes."

Josiah felt his eyes sting. He looked down at his hat so no one would notice, blinking hard. When he raised his head again, Gran was watching him with that same steady kindness that had held her family together through a hundred sorrows.

"You'd be doing us a favor," she said softly.

He grasped her hand, caressing it with his own. "Then surely, I will join you. I'll be more than honored."

Gran reached out and patted his arm once, firm and sure, the way a mother steadies a grown son who's forgotten he's allowed to lean.

Red was over by the doors now, holding Keri's coat for her, Karl waiting

114

with the quiet patience of a man who knows some things can't be rushed. Josiah walked toward them, hat still crushed in one hand. When he reached the little group, he stopped and looked at Red—really looked at him, eye to eye—for the first time since the graveside.

"I hear you make coffee strong enough to float a horseshoe," Josiah said, and the faintest smile tugged at the corner of his mouth, tremulous but real.

Red gave a short nod, something unreadable passing between them, man to man, both of them missing the same presence that wouldn't be in the room anymore.

As they moved together to turn out the lights, Josiah paused at the door and looked back once at the empty pulpit, the flowers already beginning to droop. His shoulders rose and fell with one deep, steadying breath.

"Thank you," he said again, to Gran, to all of them, to the quiet sanctuary itself. "For not letting me eat alone with that empty chair."

Then he stepped out into the cold November dusk with the family, walking a little closer to them than he had when he arrived, his hat finally back on his head but held there by a hand that no longer needed to keep turning it.

CHAPTER TEN

In the Light of the Manger

The wind off the Missouri had teeth, but the sun rode high and white, turning the snow-crusted boardwalks into glittering paths. Three days before Christmas, the streets bustled with fur caps and wool mufflers, the jingle of trace chains and the muffled thud of boots. Karl, Keri, and Gran stepped down from the sleigh in front of the First Dakota Bank, breath fogging like incense. Gran's black shawl was pinned snugly around her shoulders and neck; Keri's cheeks bloomed rose-red from the cold; Karl carried a small, mysterious bundle wrapped in brown paper.

Inside, the bank smelled of coal oil, ink, and a sharp resinous wood scent enhanced by the inviting heat filling the fairly new pine building. The cast-iron coal stove sitting in the middle of the room glowed with lump-coal embers that occasionally snapped and popped. A sweet-oily chemical smell from the kerosene lamps hung in the air, mixed with the burnt-sugar smell of melted wax sealing essential documents. Counters gleamed with wood polish and lemon oil, and behind the teller window was a hint of "new money" metal and paper aroma.

Tellers scratched ledgers behind brass bars, peering curiously at the customers.

"We're here to see Josiah—Mr. Raskin." Karl peered back at the teller, who looked up from his desk, spectacles glinting, surprise softening the stern lines of his face.

"He's in," the teller said, pointing toward the office door bearing the "J. B. Raskin" nameplate.

As they stepped into the office, Josiah rose, his chair scraping across the floor. "Karl! Ladies - come in! To what do I owe the honor?"

Karl extended his hand to Josiah. "We don't want to interrupt you," he said. "But we wanted to invite you to join us for Christmas dinner at our house. Noon sharp on the twenty-fifth. We won't take no for an answer."

116

Josiah's eyes widened, then crinkled. "I'd be honored. My housekeeper asked to have the day to be with her own family, and I couldn't refuse her." He chuckled, the sound rusty but genuine. "I'll bring a plum pudding from the hotel kitchen."

Gran reached across the desk and patted his hand. "Bring yourself, Josiah. That's gift enough."

"And your gracious hospitality will be mine," he replied.

"This will be a special day for me and Keri," Karl said. "We have been married less than six months. This will be our first Christmas as husband and wife."

Keri's cheeks, already pink from the cold, deepened a shade. She looked up at Karl, then at Josiah, her eyes shining.

"It feels like the whole world has been turned upside down and right-side up again this year," she said softly. "The flood took almost everything we owned, and blizzards claimed Karl's and Gran's ranch. We all lost family, and we all gained a new understanding of God's grace." Her voice trembled, but only for a moment.

Karl's arm tightened around her. "The Lord hasn't given us everything we thought we wanted—no easy road. But He has given us everything we need, he gave us each other, and Pa's legacy of grace . . ."

Josiah's spectacles had slipped down his nose; he did not push them back up. He simply waited, sensing there was more.

Karl drew a slow breath. "I've known since James' death that the Lord was pointing me toward the pulpit—whether that means teaching Sunday school to Norwegian children who only know three English words, or feeding whoever knocks on the door after a storm passes, or simply praying through the nights when the sermons won't come."

Keri smiled. "I'm just beginning to learn how to be a preacher's wife, but I'm eager to start practicing."

Gran reached over and patted Josiah's hand where it rested on the desk. "And that's why we're here, Josiah. This first Christmas feels like the beginning of everything God has promised us. We want to mark it by opening our home and our table to the people He's already set in our path. We'd be honored if you'd come and sit with us on Christmas Day—noon sharp—and let us serve you."

Josiah cleared his throat twice before he found his voice.

"Well," he said at last, the word rough, "I reckon a man would have to be

117

even harder-hearted than me to say no to an invitation like that."

Keri's smile broke wide and bright as sunrise on snow. "Then it's settled. Bring your appetite and your stories. We have plenty of both goose and grace to go around."

Karl extended his hand across the desk. "Merry Christmas, Josiah. The first of many, Lord willing."

Josiah clasped it firmly, then surprised them all by keeping hold long enough to add, "And may the Lord bless the ministry that begins at your table this Christmas Day. I'll be there. Wouldn't miss the start of something so blessed for all the gold in the Black Hills."

Outside, the wind still bit at their cheeks, but inside the little circle of four souls standing in the warm lamplight of the bank, it already felt like Christmas had begun.

"We'll let you get back to work," Karl said as the three made their way to the door.

The cold met them like a slap as the heavy bank door thumped shut behind them. The street was a churned-up mess of frozen mud ruts, scattered straw, and already-gray snow tinged with coal soot and hoof traffic. Every few minutes, a freight wagon, buggy, or saddle horse swept by, harness and sleigh bells jingling in the crisp air.

Every stovepipe in town belched woodsmoke, and the fragrance of boiling coffee and frying bacon drifted out the doors of the St. Charles hotel. Someone across the street was splitting kindling with a viscous thwack-thwack-thwack. They stopped to watch two carpenters on ladders nailing fresh pine garlands over the entrance of the hotel.

"Keri? Keri Miller?"

Keri froze, mittened hand flying to her chest as if to protect her heart. She knew that voice. She hadn't heard it in four years, but there was no mistaking it. She turned to view a tall, thin man in a travel-stained greatcoat, beaver hat askew. His graying beard was kept short and impeccably neat (no longer than three-quarters of an inch), trimmed straight across the bottom in a precise horizontal line that followed the hard edge of his jaw. The mustache was fuller than the rest, brushed outward and slightly downward at the corners of his mouth in the old military fashion, giving his face an even more severe, almost architectural severity. Along the cheeks, the beard thinned just enough to reveal the sharp bones beneath, and at the throat, it stopped abruptly in a perfect, ruler-straight line well above his collar, as though even the hair dared not trespass beyond the bounds he allowed it. His eyes—pale gray, sharp as winter sky—locked on hers.

"Grandfather?" The word left her lips trembling.

Arthur Miller stepped forward. Even exhausted from the stagecoach journey, standing a full six feet three in his polished knee-high boots, it was his posture, rather than sheer height, that made people notice him first. At sixty-two, he carried himself ramrod-straight, shoulders squared as if still wearing the dark-blue lieutenant's coat he had worn through the last year of his military service. Years of measuring calico and weighing coffee had not thickened his frame; he remained almost cadaverously thin, the black broadcloth frock coat hanging from his narrow shoulders like a judge's robe. His hair, once the color of ripe wheat, had gone the white of fresh-planed pine boards, combed straight back from a high, unwrinkled forehead and kept in place with a trace of European macassar oil that caught the lamplight when he turned his head.

His face was long and angular, the cheekbones sharp enough to cast faint shadows even in soft light. A neatly trimmed beard, more silver than white, framed a mouth that rarely smiled in public and, when it did, offered only the briefest upward twitch at one corner—an expression most clerks interpreted as permission to exhale. The eyes were the coldest part of him: pale gray, set deep beneath heavy brows, steady and unblinking, the color of winter river ice just before it breaks. Customers swore those eyes could count the pennies in your pocket without seeming to leave the page of the ledger in front of him.

He spoke softly, always, in a measured baritone that carried farther than most men's shouts. A single raised eyebrow or the quiet repetition of a price was enough to end any attempt at haggling. In the store, he was invariably polite—"Ma'am," "Sir," "Certainly"—but the words arrived wrapped in frost. Children were told in whispers that Mr. Miller could hear a lie from twenty paces and that his silence was heavier than most men's scolding.

Yet every December, he closed the store an hour early on Christmas Eve, hung a sprig of mistletoe above the door himself (reaching it without a stool), and handed out striped candy sticks to any child brave enough to meet his gaze. On those rare occasions, the gray eyes softened for the length of a heartbeat, and the tall, austere figure seemed almost human before the reserve settled back over him like a perfectly tailored coat.

He moved toward Keri, placing his long, thin, gloved hands lightly on her shoulders, as though she might break. "You've grown into a young woman. I've heard all sorts of reports about what's happened here since the flood ravaged Yankton. Figured it was time for me to come here and see for myself." He paused and looked at Karl and Gran, who stood next to Keri, stunned and silent. "Your friends?"

Keri moved to Karl, slipping her arm around his waist. "My husband Karl Richmond and his grandmother, Gran. They came here from Wyoming right after the flood. They were my salvation after Pa—" She hesitated. "Passed. He died almost two weeks after the flood. Karl and I married in June."

Arthur's pale complexion turned even more ashen. "The news about James is true, then. I was hoping—"

Karl draped his arm over Keri's shoulders. "Keri endured a great deal after the flood with the loss of her father and nearly losing the homestead."

Arthur stared at them silently for a tense moment. "I'm sorry you had to endure all that. And congratulations on your wedding. May I buy you all dinner at the hotel? I took a room here after getting in on the morning stagecoach."

Keri silently turned to Karl, who searched her face before answering, "Yes, sir, we'd be much obliged to join you."

As they made their way to the hotel dining room, Keri's thoughts raced. Why was Arthur really here? Would he cause trouble between her and Karl, her and Gran? Would he ridicule Pa in front of everyone? Should she trust him at all? What about Christmas Day?

Inside the St. Charles dining room, the air smelled of roast goose, sage dressing, and cedar garlands. A small tree stood in the corner, strung with popcorn and paper chains. The fire crackled in a stone hearth big enough to stand in.

They were shown to a table by the window. Keri sat stiffly, hands knotted in her lap, staring at the red-checkered cloth as though it might offer answers. The waitress set down bowls of oyster stew and a platter of fresh bread. Steam curled up, fragrant and inviting, but Keri's stomach was a hard knot.

Arthur removed his gloves with deliberate care, folding them beside his plate. For a long moment, no one spoke.

Gran, bless her, reached for the bread first. "Mr. Miller, you must be half-frozen after that stage ride. Eat while it's hot."

Keri's eyes widened as Arthur obeyed Gran's direction, tearing a piece

120

of bread with thin, precise fingers. When he tasted the stew, the faintest softening touched the corners of his mouth. Keri watched him covertly. The grandfather she remembered had never eaten in public without finding fault with something. Yet here he was, silent, almost gentle.

Karl asked a question about the roads from Sioux City. Arthur answered in full sentences, voice low, asking in turn about the homestead, the horses, the new barn. Each courteous question felt like a test, and Keri's heart hammered. Will he think Karl simple because he speaks plainly? Will he sneer at all the things we're so proud of?

But Arthur only nodded, eyes on Karl's face as though truly listening.

The dining room was warm and loud with the clatter of silverware and the low murmur of travelers, but at their small table by the window, the air felt suddenly thin, as though the four of them had stepped into a separate, fragile world.

Arthur Miller set his spoon down with deliberate care, the oyster stew barely touched. He folded his long, thin hands on the red-checkered cloth and looked at Keri—not the quick, measuring glance he usually allowed the world, but a long, unguarded stare that made her heart flutter.

"Keri," he began, voice low enough that Karl and Gran had to lean in to hear, "I didn't come all this way just to see how you'd weathered the flood." He paused, the muscle in his jaw working beneath the silver beard. "You are the only family I have left."

The words fell between them like stones into still water.

Arthur's gaze dropped to his plate. "When your father—my son—turned down my offer to take over the store and carried you off to—here, I told him never to darken my door again. I meant it. I was proud." He paused, drawing in a deep breath. "And I was wrong. I built a wall of silence taller than any man could climb, and I have lived inside it for the last four years." His fingers tightened until the knuckles blanched. "I always thought stubbornness was strength. Turns out it's only a longer way to die alone."

Keri felt the blood leave her face. The room tilted; the laughter from another table sounded miles away. A storm roared inside her head:

He regrets it. Four years. He's asking to be let back in. What do I say? What would Pa want me to say? What would Jesus say?

Her breath came shallow and quick. She gripped the edge of the table to steady herself.

Arthur lifted his eyes again—pale winter ice, shimmering now with

121

something dangerously close to tears. "I don't deserve anything from you, child. I know that. But if we could at least be civil . . . if you would allow an old man the mercy of a letter now and then, a line at Christmas . . . I would count that a greater gift than I have any right to expect."

Silence.

Gran reached for Keri's hand under the table and squeezed once—steady, steady.

Keri swallowed hard, searching for the words that felt bigger than herself, words that came from somewhere deeper than her own hurt.

"Grandfather," she said, and her voice trembled but did not break, "I'm so glad you came." She saw the faint flicker of surprise in his face.

"Family means everything to me," she continued, the sentences tumbling out as if afraid they would be snatched away. "And I want you to know—you are welcome at the homestead anytime. The door will never be closed to you. Not for supper, not for a night, not for a month of Sundays if you want it. We have an extra room, and Gran makes the best coffee on the Missouri River. And we all want you to be with us on Christmas Day." She glanced sideways at Karl and Gran, hoping to determine if she had gone too far.

A tiny, wondering smile tugged at the corner of Arthur's mouth—barely there, but real.

Keri leaned forward, tears brimming now. "And we most certainly will exchange letters. I want you to know what the horses are doing, and how the garden grows, and every silly thing that happens. I want you to know us. And I want to know you." She reached across the table and laid her small, work-rough hand over his thin, cold one.

"Because God is big on second chances, on grace, Grandfather. And so am I."

Arthur stared at their joined hands as though he had never seen such a thing before. Then, very slowly, his fingers turned and closed around hers—lightly at first, then with a grip that trembled.

"Thank you, Keri," he whispered, the words rough as gravel. "Thank you."

Across the table Karl's eyes were bright; Gran dabbed at her cheeks with the corner of her napkin and pretended it was only the steam from the stew.

Outside, the snow kept falling, soft and forgiving, covering the raw little town in a quilt of grace.

Inside, an old wall cracked, and light—long delayed—came pouring through.

The homestead lay hushed under a foot of new snow, the amber lights in the windows of the house casting gold-tinted shapes across the snow. Inside, Gran had worked miracles.

Rising before dawn, wrapped in two shawls against the cold, she turned the plain sitting room into something of a storybook. Pine boughs draped every beam; their sharp, sweet scent filled the air and mingled with the richer smells of the feast: roast goose browning in the cast-iron Dutch oven, sage-and-onion stuffing, potatoes boiled with rosemary from last summer's dried bunch, wild cranberry sauce tart and bright, and a lofty loaf of whole wheat bread rising on the back of the stove. She had even found three red ribbons somewhere and tied them around the tin cups at each place, a touch so small and so Gran that Keri's eyes stung when she saw it.

By eleven o'clock, the guests arrived—Josiah Raskin in his Sunday broadcloth, carrying the promised plum pudding wrapped in a clean white napkin. Arthur Miller, almost taller than the doorway, brushed snow from his beaver hat with careful precision. Red came in last, hanging his hat with all the others and making the rounds to shake hands, hug Keri and Gran, and wish all a merry Christmas.

"I smelled Gran's bread half a mile off," Red said with a half-smile, "but truth is, I came for the company more than the victuals."

The table was crowded but perfect. Karl had planed an extra leaf into it the week before; the oilcloth was scrubbed snowy clean, and Gran's one set of china plates—saved from her own wedding—shone in the lamplight.

The goose crackled when Karl carved it; the skin was mahogany and crisp, the meat beneath fragrant with woodsmoke from the apple-wood fire. They ate slowly, reverently. Every bite tasted of stubborn love and hope.

Conversation started politely—weather, the price of wheat, the need for a bridge across the Missouri—but after the plates were heaped a second time, the talk drifted deeper.

Josiah set down his fork and stared into the fire a long moment.

"My Maggie has been gone twelve years this January," he said quietly. "Some mornings I still wake in the morning and expect her to be there."

Arthur's head came up sharply, gray eyes startled, as though someone had spoken a secret he thought only he carried.

123

"Twenty-one years for me," he answered, voice barely above the crackle of the stove. "Martha took fever in '59. I buried her in the spring thaw and have measured every day against that one ever since."

Keri glanced at Karl; Gran's eyes were wide and shining. Neither man had ever spoken of his wife in public, and here they were laying their loneliness bare like an offering.

Josiah went on, softer still. "I was hard as flint after Maggie died. Angry at God I suppose. Thought faith was for women and children. Then came Alex—his heartfelt confession about how sin had twisted his soul and his life. Such a genuine confession. Such a transformed heart and concern for others." Josiah's voice cracked. "It was his willingness to reveal his broken heart that changed mine overnight. That and his sincere plea for others to accept God's grace."

"I reckon losin' a wife is about the hardest thing the Lord ever asks of a man this side of glory," Red said. "Some mornings I still reach across the bed as if Bess will be there. Yet, as dark as some days have been, I know where she and my young 'uns are. I want to give God the glory for bringin' me through the hard times. And I know I'll see all of them again, whole and happy, when my own work here is done. That promise, that's the gift I take out and unwrap anew every single Christmas."

Gran pressed her hand to her heart. "Bless you, Red. The Lord is faithful. No matter what path our life takes, there is always hope."

Arthur sat quietly, turning his coffee cup slowly in his big hands. At last, he cleared his throat.

"Martha was always one for reading her Bible, morning and night," he said. "I never could quite understand what she found in those pages that made her eyes shine so."

"Have you spent much time reading God's word?" Karl asked.

Arthur shook his head. "No. I was always too busy tending the store. All my life I thought I knew everything that was needful to be happy."

He gave a short, sad laugh and looked around the table, his gaze settling on Keri.

"Turns out I missed the most important things. I'm seeing now, sitting here amongst you today, that the greatest gifts he ever set before me weren't a successful business and a full purse or a grand house. They were the folks sitting round this table right now—and the ones already waiting for us on the other side."

124

Karl leaned forward, his voice tender. "Arthur, it sounds as though your Martha learned to love God with all her heart. And the place we come to know him, to love him, is in his word."

Arthur turned his gaze to Karl as the word began penetrating the hardness that had so long captured his heart.

"I think I see now that the real treasures were the people the Lord put in my life," he said. "You all—this family—have shown his mercy to me. Turns out happiness isn't something you chase down; it's sitting right beside you when you finally open your eyes."

Red lifted his cup in a toast. "To the gifts that rust can't corrupt and death can't steal."

"Amen, and amen!" Gran said as they all joined in the gesture.

Silence settled, warm and healing.

After the pudding—smooth, rich, dark—Karl fetched his Bible from the shelf. Its leather cover was cracked and soft as cloth. They pushed the dishes aside and gathered close while Karl read the old words by lamplight:

"And she brought forth her firstborn son, and wrapped him in swaddling clothes, and laid him in a manger . . ."

Arthur sat motionless, eyes fixed on some middle distance, lips moving almost imperceptibly with the familiar verses. When Karl reached "Glory to God in the highest, and on earth peace, goodwill toward men," a single tear slipped down the old man's angular cheek and disappeared into his silver beard.

The fire was crackling low as Karl stood with the old family Bible open in his hands, his voice steady and tender.

Arthur had been quiet for a long while after the coffee was poured a second time. He sat straight-backed in Karl's homemade chair, obviously lost in thought. The fire popped; snow tapped the single windowpane. At last, he cleared his throat, the sound rough, almost reluctant.

"I have spent forty-two years," he said, voice low but carrying in the small room the way it once carried across a crowded store floor, "believing that a man's worth was measured by the weight of his ledgers and the shine on his counter."

He stared across the room, images only he could see passing before him. "I kept the store open twelve hours a day, six days a week, fifty-two weeks a year. Closed only on Sunday because the town expected it, and on Christmas Day because even I wasn't fool enough to fight that battle. I told myself I

125

was building something—security, respect, a name that would outlast me." A faint, bitter smile touched the corner of his mouth and vanished.

"Turns out all I built was a very fine, very empty house. The shelves are full. The rooms are silent. The only footsteps I hear at night are my own, echoing like a stranger's."

He lifted his eyes—those winter-gray eyes that had once made clerks tremble—and let them rest on Keri, then Karl, then Gran.

"I counted every penny that came in, and I never once counted the years going out. I thought profit was the same as purpose." His fingers tightened on the journal. "I was wrong. Dead wrong. A store can be rebuilt after a fire or a flood. A family . . . once you drive it off, it doesn't always come back."

His gaze settled on Keri again, softer now, almost pleading.

"You offered me something today worth more than every dollar I ever earned. You offered me a place at this table, a chair by this fire, a chance to be more than the man who locked the door on his own son."

He drew a slow, shaky breath.

"I don't know how to be anything else yet. But if you'll let me sit here a little longer . . . if you'll let me write letters to you now and then . . . maybe I can learn what really matters before the ledger closes for good."

Then, so quietly they almost missed it, he added, "I've kept the store long enough. It's time I opened the door to something that lasts."

Josiah left first, sleigh bells fading into the dusk. Then Karl walked out to check the stock, giving Arthur a moment alone with the Keri and Gran. He stood by the door, hat in hand, coat buttoned to the throat.

"Keri," he began, then stopped. He cleared his throat once, twice. "May I . . . would you permit your grandfather a hug?"

The words came out rough, almost fearful.

Keri's eyes swam. "Yes, of course." She stepped into his arms. "I love you, Grandfather."

For one heartbeat, he was stiff as a fence post; then his arms came around her, thin but surprisingly strong, and he held her as though she were the only solid thing left in his world. She felt the tremor in his shoulders, the damp of tears against her hair. He stood stiffly next to the door, pulling on his gloves, snow swirling into the kitchen as he cracked the door, ready to leave.

Gran stepped forward with a folded quilt over her arm—a bright Log Cabin pattern, one she finished just days ago.

"You've got a long cold ride back to town," she said matter-of-factly.

"Take this. It's warm, and it's built from the scraps of three generations of Richmonds from Wyoming. It'll see you through many nights." Arthur started to protest.

"I couldn't—I have blankets at the hotel—"

But Gran was already tucking it under his arm. Her hand brushed his as she withdrew it, and she allowed her hand to remain a moment longer than necessary. "I'll bring it back," he said, his voice rougher than usual. Gran looked up at him, snowflakes lighting in her white hair like stars. "See that you do, Arthur Miller," she answered softly. "I'll be waiting."

She closed the door gently after him, but not before Keri caught the faintest curve of a smile on her lips and a look in her eyes that Keri hadn't seen there before.

Gran pulled Keri down beside her on the high-backed wooden storage bench used for keeping wood handy for the fire . The fire popped softly; the scent of pine and goose still hung in the air.

"He's terrified, child," Gran said gently. "Terrified of hope. Men like your grandfather build walls out of pride and grief, and when someone hands them a door, they don't know whether to walk through or bolt it shut."

Keri wiped her eyes with her apron. "How do I show him God loves him, Gran? And that I do too?"

Gran thought for a long moment, rocking slowly.

"You already started. You let him hold you. From now on, you write him a letter every week and tell him about the homestead, the horses, the silly things the colts do—ordinary life, full of grace. You invite him for spring planting, for summer berry-picking, for every small thing. Love isn't a sermon, Keri. It's a chair pulled up to the fire and a cup of coffee poured without asking. Day after day. That's how walls come down—one brick at a time, carried away by someone who refuses to leave."

Outside, the prairie lay white and still under a sky full of stars. Inside, the little sod cabin smelled of Christmas fulfilled, and Keri fell asleep believing, for the first time in years, that some miracles arrive wearing an old man's frost-rimmed beard and carrying countless years of sorrow in their eyes.

127

CHAPTER ELEVEN

Testing the Road of Grace

The letter came on an iron-gray winter morning when the wind prowled around the eaves like a wolf that had not been fed.

As soon as he picked it up at the general store, Karl was struck by the single blue envelope addressed in a hand he didn't recognize. It captured his imagination all the way home. He slit it open by the stove while the coffee boiled, expecting a late Christmas greeting.

He read it once, quickly. He read it again, slowly, the paper trembling between his fingers.

Gran looked up from her mending. "Bad news, Karl?"

Karl's voice came out thin. "From Elias Jorgensen. Says I've gone soft on sin. Says letting Pa confess in front of the congregation and then welcoming him back like nothing happened makes a mockery of holiness. Says if adultery and fathering a child out of wedlock can be washed away with a few tears, then what's the point of the Law at all." He folded the letter with deliberate care, but his knuckles were white. "He's leaving the church. Taking his family with him."

The words hung in the air like frost.

Karl walked to the window and stared out at the frozen prairie. "What if he's right, Gran? Was I too quick to embrace Pa? Maybe real repentance needs . . . more time. More suffering. I'm not sure."

Gran laid her needle aside and came to stand behind him, small hand on his broad back.

"Karl Richmond, you listen to me. When your father wept, shoulders shaking and his voice breaking, telling all of us the worst thing he'd ever done; when he named the sin, named the boy, named the shame he'd carried for so many years; do you remember what you felt?"

Karl closed his eyes. "Shock. That wasn't the father I had known. Then sorrow, to know he carried that by himself for so long. And a love and

129

respect for him I never felt before. One that's rooted in my gratitude for what God has done for me."

"And when he insisted on sharing it with everyone in church because he thought it might help someone else? You didn't wait for him to earn forgiveness and healing. You didn't demand he crawl. You just loved him the way the Father loved him." Gran's voice grew fierce with tenderness. "That, Karl, is the gospel. Not a scale that weighs how much pain a man endures before he's allowed back in the house. Grace isn't grace if it keeps accounts."

Karl's breath clouded the window glass. "But what if other members of the congregation think we're excusing sin?"

"Karl, listen to an old woman who has buried a husband and a son. Jesus himself was called a friend of publicans and sinners because he dared to eat with them before they had cleaned themselves up. The Pharisees spat the same words Elias wrote: 'This man receiveth sinners.' And Jesus answered by telling them about a father who ran—ran, mind you—to a boy still stinking of the pigpen."

"That's true," Karl agreed.

"We knew your pa's repentance was genuine. You saw his face when he finally dared to confess. You heard the screams that tore out of him in the night, and you saw the peace that came when he knew he was forgiven. And Alex himself begged to tell the whole church, not to clear his name, but so that others might taste the same mercy before they wandered as far as he did."

Gran took a deep breath and a moment to gauge Karl's response to her counsel.

"In my lifetime, I have watched good people carry secret failures for decades because they were too afraid of the Elias Jorgensens of this world to ever confess them," she said. "So, who knows how the Lord will yet use your father's broken story to open prison doors no man can see? Who knows what soul, even now hiding in shame, will hear of a church that opened its arms instead of its ledger book and will dare to come home?"

She squeezed his arm. "Even so, it seems wise to give the congregation a chance to speak. Let every heart be heard. A shepherd does not lead in silence."

The following Sunday, the little log church was packed tight again, men standing along the walls, women with babies on their laps. Word had traveled faster than the wind.

After the singing and the Scripture, Karl stepped forward, the blue

130

envelope in his hand.

"Brethren," he began, voice steady though his heart pounded, "most of you already know that Elias Jorgensen and his family will not worship with us again. They believe I acted hastily when my father confessed his great sin before you, and I received him at once with joy. Elias believes we should have waited, watched, and required more proof that his repentance was genuine.

"I will not stand here and say Elias is completely wrong to care about holiness. But I will say this: I knew my father. Some of you heard of the cries that came from his room in the nights before he confessed. If you could have seen his face the morning grace found him. If you had seen the relief, the holy terror, the grief for those he wounded, and the longing to keep even one more person from receiving God's grace and mercy, you could not have answered him with anything but love."

The church was absolutely silent, save for the occasional whimper or whisper of a small child.

"I may yet be mistaken," Karl continued. "I am young and still learning. But I know without a doubt that, had it not been for my brother James, who shared the gospel at every opportunity and died in my arms, encouraging me to trust God, I would not stand before you today. God took what was meant for destruction and darkness and used it for good. I believe he's just started using it for good. In the deepest part of my heart, I believe Pa's sorrow was true sorrow, and his turning was true turning. I do not wish to cause division among us. So, I lay the matter before you openly. If any man or woman believes we ought to have done differently, stand now and speak, and point us to the Scriptures that teach a better way. Let us reason together in the fear of God."

A hush fell so complete they could hear the stove ticking in the corner.

Then old Hans Larson rose slowly, joints creaking. "Pastor Karl, I sat right there the Sunday you read our Pa's letter. From what I heard, I believe a dead man came to life. I say we did what the Bible says: 'If he repents, forgive him.' I move we keep on forgiving, keep on preaching grace, and keep on praying the Jorgensens find it too."

Young Anders Swenson stood next, cap in hand. "My own brother ran off to the gold fields, living wild. I been praying he'll come home one day. If he does, I want him to know there's a church where the father runs to meet him. I stand with you, Pastor."

No other man rose. A few women dabbed at their eyes.

After the final hymn and prayer, while folks pulled on coats and scarves, a bent elder named Olaf Petersen made his way forward. His beard was whiter than the snow outside, and his eyes still sharp as a hawk's.

He placed a gnarled hand on Karl's shoulder.

"Young Karl, the Lord is going to do a mighty work through you. I see it. A man who can stand in the storm and still ask, 'Have I done wrong?' instead of shouting, 'I am right!'—that is a man the Spirit can trust with much."

Karl's eyes filled. "Brother Olaf, even that humility is not my own. It is the amazing grace of God that teaches a man to bend. Once we have received such mercy, how can we measure it out with a teaspoon to the next sinner?"

Olaf smiled, teeth still strong at eighty. "Keep giving it away by the barrel, son. That's how the world will know we belong to Jesus."

He shuffled out into the cold, and Karl stood alone a moment in the quiet church, the scent of pine knots and candle smoke lingering in the air.

Outside, the wind still blew hard across the Dakota prairie, but inside Karl's heart something settled, quiet and sure.

Because of grace, the door stayed open. Because of grace, the feast was spread for anyone who would come. Because of grace, even the leaving of one family could not close the arms of the church that had learned to run.

The house was quiet, the wind worn out at last. Only the faint tick of the kitchen clock drifted up through the floorboards and the occasional crackle from the banked stove downstairs.

In their small bedroom, the cold pressed against the walls like a living thing, but under three quilts and a buffalo robe, Karl and Keri lay warm, pressed close to stay warm. Moonlight, thin and pearl-bright, slipped between the frost feathers on the windowpane and laid a soft silver wash across the bed.

Karl found Keri's hand beneath the covers and laced his fingers through hers.

"Keri," he whispered into the dark, "while I was speaking this morning, the Lord settled something deep inside me. I have been given great, staggering grace, not a drop of it earned, not a breath of it deserved. Just poured out because God loved us. And he showed me plain: there will be more Elias Jorgensens in the years ahead. Hard men, certain men, measuring men. In those times, above all else, we must remember that God desires to bless them with grace, too, if they'll have it."

132

Keri's fingers tightened around his. "When I think how far the Lord reached to bring the two of us together, across years and miles and heartbreak, only God could have done it. If he can redeem all of that, he can redeem even the Elias Jorgensens."

Karl gave a quiet chuckle, then pushed himself up, leaning back against the log headboard. He tugged the quilts higher around their shoulders as Keri sat up beside him, her hair loose and brushing his cheek.

Moonlight bathed them both, turning the rough quilt to mother-of-pearl, making the small room feel suddenly vast and hushed, like the inside of a seashell.

Karl's voice dropped even lower. "One more thing he told me today. You and I must stay close. Closer than breath. We will need each other's hand to hold, each other's prayers to cover us, each other's laughter to keep us sane."

Keri turned to him, eyes shining in the moon-glow. "Staying close to you will never be hard, Karl Richmond. Every morning, I wake astonished that the Lord saw fit to bring you to me."

He smiled, the teasing note she loved creeping in. "Careful, Mrs. Richmond. A fellow might get proud, hearing that every night."

"Then let him," she whispered, and leaned in, and kissed him, slow and sweet and warm.

When they parted, she shivered, teeth chattering once, and burrowed back down into the nest of blankets. Karl followed, pulling her against his chest, one arm tucked securely around her.

He spoke into her hair, voice husky with wonder.

"If the Lord ever blesses us with a little girl, curled up small and warm like her mama, what would you think of calling her Grace?"

Keri stilled, then gave a soft, wondering laugh that was half a sob.

"I would think," she said, pressing his hand over her heart, "that it is the most perfect name in all the world."

Outside, the Dakota night lay deep and white and silent. Inside, two hearts beat steady under the same quilt, kept warm by the same stubborn, reckless, astonishing love that learned how to run down a road to meet a prodigal. Because of grace.

Nestled in rural Yankton, South Dakota, Loretta Sorensen weaves tales of faith, love, and resilience inspired by the windswept Dakota prairies that have been her lifelong home. With her husband, Alan, she has raised Belgian draft horses for over 50 years, a passion that's woven throughout her inspirational Christian prairie romance series. Her stories blend the rugged beauty of 1880s Dakota Territory with heartfelt journeys of hope, drawing readers into a world where God's grace shines through life's challenges.

A freelance journalist for over 35 years, Loretta's work has graced *Progressive Farmer, Farm Journal*, and GRIT Magazine, capturing the heart of rural America. She holds degrees from Mount Marty University and South Dakota State University, and is pursuing Biblical Studies at Michigan's Christian Leadership Institute, infusing her writing with spiritual depth. Through her company, Prairie Hearth Publishing, LLC, founded in 2005, she has published works like *30 Dakota Prairie Bread Recipes, A Marriage Designed by God*, and *It's Your Time To Fly*, and supported over 20 indie authors. *These Dakota Dreams* is the first novel in her Dakota Dreams Series.

When not writing, Loretta paints, quilts, gardens, and serves her community through prison ministry. Follow her on BookBub for updates on her romance series, and visit www.lorettasorensenbooks. com to learn about her latest titles or go to her YouTube channel, "Our Dakota Horse Tales," to glimpse the prairie life that fuels her stories. On Facebook, look for Dakota Prairie Romance - Loretta Sorensen and connect at dakotaprairieromance@gmail.com.

www.ingramcontent.com/pod-product-compliance
Lightning Source LLC
Chambersburg PA
CBHW051847170626
46807CB00003B/1387